The smell of cigarette smoke repulses me. The smoke cast a

fog so thick it can be cut with a knife. I feel suffocated in the

stagnated stench of wet filters and burning tobacco. I stay planted

to my seat as if my legs were growing roots to the floor. Standing

tall front and center, a man is speaking, teaching from a book. As he

explains the meanings of each paragraph, I start daydreaming losing

interest in the seventh step of recovery. He may not be your cup of

tea, but to me he is my tall drink of water. I have remembered

every word he has ever spoke in the front of this room. Verbatim.

He is my everything. Except for a minor technicality, he does not

even know I exist. His glasses bring a distinguished charm to his

face. His hair line tells a story of a man who has seen his fair share

of troubles. He towers over a lectern. His stature sends a message

of importance. His voice projects throughout the room. No

microphone needed. His words roll off his tongue with knowledge

and so much power. I am enchanted each time I attend a meeting

1

where he is the speaker. I may be daydreaming about our tiny little cottage home filled with books. Yet, his words stick with me. He uses no slang and his Appalachian accent vanishes into each well spoken sentence.

He wraps up the meeting. Time for coffee, which I hate the bitterness taste of. Time for pastries which I never would eat in front of him or anyone else in here. This is the time for endless chatter. We congregate to gossip about the people who are no longer in attendance and violate most every other policy set in place for this program. People pair up passing out numbers for sponsorship. I stand in the back gazing at him like he is...Thanksgiving dinner. I am hungry for his touch. I wish I was at a bar because then making my presence known would not feel so awkward. It is not alcohol that I crave, it's the atmosphere. The companionship of others with failed hopes and dreams like mine. The ambience of the freedom of fun. These meetings are held in church basements. I can not cuss in here. I was raised to do better than that. I was also raised better than to live in a homeless shelter. Yet, here I am. Currently on parole after serving 367 days of my one-ten year sentence. Being on parole is also a hinderance to my freedom. My logic tells me someone like him would never give someone like me a second look, but my heart tells me a whole different story and I continue to daydream of sharing a cottage style home with him.

The meeting is over and the crowded room is down to just a few, discussing work, religion and politics no subject that I could care less about, yet here I stand pretending that is the small of my back he is escorting through the door, like he is doing her. He pops up the umbrella and escorts his woman to her beige Mercedes. I wish my little cousin Jewel, was here to see this car. All I can recognize is the Mercedes emblem but she could see the car and know instantly if it is a cheap one or the most expensive. Then she would give a whole life story based on make and model of car. If she had not submitted to a life of crime she would have most definitely been successful as an FBI profiler. She would never be caught dead in one of these meetings even when she was court ordered to attend. She knew someone who signed her paper that said she was progressing steadily in her recovery. Things tend to work out more easily for attractive people. I have watched her breeze through circumstances that would kill others. Sterling reaches for the door and opens it for Phyllis. She is certainly quite capable of opening her own door, and popping up her own umbrella. Phyllis is a geriatric physician. Rumor has it that she has saved more lives than she has lost. I do not believe one word of that mere gossip. She is a doctor, of course people are going to say nice things about her in hopes for free health care. Especially in this lack of health insurance environment. Phyllis, is a thin, tall blonde. Her tiny physique looks like she has spent a lifetime on a vegan diet. I bet she is one of those people that add raisins to the potato salad. I have never met nobody personally that does that, but I have heard rumors about people that do. Other than an awesome career and questionable car, being tiny and blonde is all she has going for her. Her face is homely and ugly. She looks like she fell out of the ugly tree and hit every branch on the way down. PLOP! SPLAT! SMUSH! Right into a life sentence with that face. Needless to say her attitude is superior. She tries to make others feel inferior to her. It could be due to the fact I have a few red neck tendencies or my jealousy, but I hate her. Her nose is turned up so far in the air that she would drown in this rain without that umbrella. For someone responsible for the care of others and have had went through all of that school, she surely did not graduate with common sense. She honestly thinks nobody can smell the hint of gin and tonic on her breath. She thinks nobody can see the flask shining in the opening of her Coach bag. I can and I do.

Thunder shakes the ground as they drive off into the dusk. Driving into the life I want to be sharing with him. Grey and pink skies dim a little bit more with each stride that I take. I walk faster to catch up with five guys who are also cohabitating in a rehab program at the shelter. Shelter rules forbid us to communicate with each other. Clearly we are adults living out childish hard headed lifestyles, so we pay no attention to the rules. We run, we laugh, on the way and divide just ahead of the parking lot in hopes that we wont get caught. Although common sense tells me that not one soul is going to be out roaming these grounds on an evening like this. The darkness fills the sky but doesn't make the rain light up one bit. As a matter of fact it is raining sideways. Cold wetness hugs my soaking clothes to my body. My wet footsteps echoes down the empty halls. The musty scent of sorrow and bad decisions permeates throughout this building. For now it is home to me. Not all of these homeless people are homeless because of addiction. Mental illness is the main reason these beds stay full. Half of the first floor is sectioned off for homeless men and the other half is for men battling the demons of their addiction. One the second and third floor of this Great Depression era building is where families are housed. In the mornings the children that live here catch the school bus at the end of the parking lot. All of the other children on the bus can see the home of the children that live here. It is heart breaking. I try to avoid bus stop times because I know what these children go through from cruel bullies on the bus. When I was younger I was bullied for years. I wanted to kill myself in the fourth grade. I hated school and my classmates. Mostly, they made me hate myself.

On the fourth floor where the winds breezes through these rattled windows is where the women residents live. We are affectionately known as the Dirty Thirty. I do not take offense to that because some of us deserve that term. Most of us do. We have more rules and less leniency than the other floors. Our recovery therapist is a haggled old lady, Susan. I am positive that in a former life she was a Nazi soldier. She lacks empathy for anyone yet she works here. There is a zero tolerance for rule breaking here. The consequence is being put out onto the street. Some of us are here because we had no other place to finish our parole. If you are paroled here like me, the consequence is violating a rule here is also in violation of parole and being sent back to prison could possibly be a consequence. My parole officer, helped me get into here a few months after I was released. Something about my dirty drug screens and my lack of stability irritated him. I only have three weeks left before my sentence is discharged.

By the time I reach the fourth floor, I am huffing, as if I am having an asthma attack. This must be what a collapsed lung feels like. Ah, the consequences of not exercising. My weight bothers me, however it does not bother me so much, that I am willing to exercise or say no to deep-fried Oreos. My body is a trophy of the generations of good cooks in my family. Our dietary beliefs are simple, deep fry it or put gravy on it. That would make anything taste good. Season your vegetables with seasoning salt and fat back. And pizza can have vegetables on it, as long as they are smothered in cheese, matter of fact extra cheese. Fruit? Yes, you must have that in your food source. I eat apples as long as they are covered in brown sugar and stewed down to the goodness. I am panting and folded over as I look down my assigned hallway. Black and brown squares reflect the walls and old closed doors. We need more rules up here because our behaviors vary from cattiness to down right vicious. Our rebellious spirits collide with different personalities like a semi truck slamming into a tree on an icy curve. Our irrational thoughts control our fear of consequences, and we test the water as many chances as we get.

The shower is vacant so I seize the opportunity to get wet once more. I have a fear of falling when I take a shower so I do not stay long enough for super effective results. I feel as though, I maintain necessary washing. My feet are attacked by the animal monsters of everyone else's hair clustered in the drain. I find this grotesquely disgusting. I cut the water off and bounce out. Eating is prohibited in our rooms. Or at least that is what the sign posted down the hall states. Yet, here I sit slouched in a floral print chair obviously donated by the family of a deceased grandmother. I am not totally disrespectful at least I am trying to silence the noise from the Doritos bag. I begin my evening reading and meditation moments. No, not the Bible. True Blood. I am infatuated with vampires. The eroticism, raises the hair on my arms. I am intrigued with page 7 so I continue to escape my reality divulging my thoughts into the words on the pages. Noises down the hall are making it hard for me to remain involved in my reading. Ms. Kelly, the most timid monitor here is on duty tonight. She treats us like we are human beings instead of the rejects of society that we are. I place True Blood by my chip bag and peep out of my door.

A melee of drama surrounds Ms.Kelly. The fear in her face is too much for me to stand here casting a quiet stare. I pounce down the hall like a Tiger winning the prize of the targeted prey. The drama is because Ms.Kelly caught four women in the bathroom smoking marijuana. Not every addict shares my moral code of accepting responsibility for their actions. Junkie code states that you always blame others for your actions. I am the exception to that rule. These gypsies, tramps and thieves have crossed the line. I hate bullies, often times I have flashbacks to when I was a child being bullied. Leg braces to keep my hips straight, overweight with telescopic eye glasses. Crowds gathered to throw rocks at me and laugh when I would fall running to get free from the groups of evil children. Evil children that I would have to sit in church with on Sundays. Somehow on Sunday morning their evilness rested as they held the hands of their parents showing off their spotless clean Sunday best outfits. The pastors hand never melted when he reached out to shake their hand. I cuff my hands over my ears because their loud yells are disrupting my peace. When that happens my brain goes out to far out dark places I can not describe. Scary thoughts seize my mind. Other voices mumbling start to interfere with my logic. Within seconds my heavy footsteps become agile. As if I am floating on a cloud.

The yells I hear now, I own them. I see nothing as if I am standing in the woods in the dead of night. Wetness drains from my knuckles to my fingers. I am panting at my loss of breath as if I am in respiratory failure. My arms feel heavier now. I am clueless to my surroundings. Yet, I keep lifting my heavy arms. Adrenaline keeps me in motion even though I am out of breath. I feel a tight grasp surrounding my arms and body. I can hear people shouting "STOP!" My spinning vision regains focus and I see Ms. Kelly running as fast as her tiny legs will carry her. I look down and see my bloody hands are holding Cheryl by the hair of her head. I tug a little tighter and feel a release as I pull wads of her hair out by the root. I raise my head up once more and notice the crowd around me. I drop her like she is a hot potato. She moans as the cold tile floor hugs her body. Every eye in the crowd is on me. I do not know what has just happened. I do not know what to do next. What do they expect me to do? I lift my size 10.5 wide foot up and slam them into Cheryls ribs. I repeat it once more, because she has upset me and mainly because the crowd is giving me more attention than ever.

I have no recollection of what just happened. I was told and told... over and over again, that I just floated down the hall and asked Cheryl politely to shut her mouth. It seems Cheryl thought she could intimidate me with vicious threats as she did Ms. Kelly. Cheryl learned a lesson today that she can not go through life assuming that everyone is going to have a war of words with her. Some people like to fight, like me. Truth is, I love to fight. I love a good bloody knock down drag out fight. Especially if I am the victor. Cheryl has some slight face swelling and I am sure she may have suffered a broken rib. I heard the snap when my jump made contact. The EMTs are loading her up now. She will be fine. As her blood rolling down the drain off of my hands, the all too familiar, unfamiliar mumbles in my mind have subsided. I do not worry nor do I fear my consequences that I will certainly face tomorrow. I may not be much for always choosing the rational or moral choice, but I am prepared to accept the consequences for any of my wrong doings. I do not feel any remorse or sympathy for Cheryl. I am unsure if what I did what right or wrong. My aunt brought back from rehab when she went the most absurd saying, "Two wrongs don't make a right." She is always reciting that foolish phrase. If someone wrongs me then I exercise my right to wrong them. There is no exceptions to that rule.

Chapter 2

Nobody plans for prison, yet I went there. Nobody plans to live in a recovery center, or homeless shelter, yet somehow I managed to do so. I also managed to get put out of there. I knew I was going to get put out after the fight. I did not plan on fighting nor do I have a plan for the aftermath. For now I am just walking. This is an unusually hot day for October. 82 degrees and sunny, which would be nice if I were walking for relaxation or hanging out. But this heat is swelling my feet like the yeast rolls my aunt makes for holiday dinners. They get heavier and heavier with each step. In these mountains the weather is just an unpredictable as the voices in my head. Sunny southern sunshine today, but two days from now snowflakes could be romanticizing in the darkness. My baby cousin, Jewel would take me in without second thought. She would feed me, probably anywhere I wanted to eat or cook me anything I wanted to eat. She would wash my clothes and make sure my pillow and blanket would smell like Gain. I could wake up in her immaculately clean house

with the smell of pancakes and Yankee candles starting my day. All

of that sounds amazing because it is. Or at least it could be.

Except for, Jewel has a husband. A hateful overbearing being of

space. Her life as well did not go as planned. She also shares the

convict status as me and a variety of our family members share. She

was a single mother of two girls until she married a beast. On

holidays her children's classroom have the most decadent desserts

for their parties. Jewel whips up bakery style desserts and adds

decorative designs according to the theme of the party. Who knew

you could take bananas and turn them into ghost? She does. She

would kill over dead before she would be the paper plate toting

mom. I have not visited her home in a while, but I see it clear in my

mind. Big bushing blooming rhoderendrens are fluffing up each

corner of her yard. A fabulous welcome wreath hangs from her

door. On the outside it looks perfect. And when you open the door,

it appears to be perfect but it is not. Her beast can not bring himself to love her children, the girls do not have his DNA therefore they are used for special effect features for them. In public you see the worlds greatest dad.

Before they were married he adored her children. She no longer lives in a shanty house on the other side of the tracks. Now, they sit high on the hillside. Jewel, is an overcomer. It never bothered her that her children's biological fathers were worthless. She stepped up, and that is all that matters. She told them that their father was in Heaven. They were a child of God. That brought tears to my eyes. I thought it was such a sweet sentiment. Jewel, was a force to be reckoned with. She ran her own business and took care of her children, prior to getting locked up. Her prison aftermath is when she married the Beast. Her girls wear the best of brands. Everything appears to have worked out well for them. It appears God blessed the broken road. All that glitters is not gold. The foundation that holds her two story brick home up has cracks in it.

Most weekends those blessed little girls go to sleep with expensive headphones, clinching their ears. They do that to drown out the vicious words he screams at their mother. They lay afraid to come downstairs in fear of what they may see him doing to their mother. It is just hateful words being exchanged. He pays all of the bills and keeps her dependent on him so that he can treat her however he pleases. I am not being partial or judgmental because she is my family. I am honest when I say she is too pretty for him. He should parade her around like a showpiece. He should take pride in even having the opportunity to even know her. He is blessed to have her as his wife. On the physical scale he should not have even got her number. Jewel is not like that, she wouldn't shun someone because of their looks. It's hard for me to believe he was even raised right. I believe that he wants to beat the pretty off of her any way he can. Her personality alone makes her deserve the best in life. So I don't understand why he would not adore her like the rest of us do.

I desire to kill him. Mostly when the family is gossiping about how stupid she is for continuing on with him. They act as though they do not understand how relationships like that work. One time she went to a women's resource center for some kind of help. They told her that they could not help women like her, all of their services were limited to women without felonies, and that she should just go pray and eventually God will open a window for her. Another time she tried to get a divorce on her own. That was unsuccessful and much embarrassing to her. The clerk told her that she had to show proof of income to qualify for indigent divorce. She explained to the clerk that the only income she has is his. She went on to say his income was too high for her qualify for other forms of government assistance. The clerk then said "well go home and tell him you need 269.00 dollars and we will get it filed when you come back." Perhaps the clerk also does not understand how relationships like theirs work. There was no way he would give her money to divorce him. She is beautiful, smart, funny and is a domestic diva. My aunt says he don't want her but don't want nobody else to have her. He is far to hateful to up and leave her

despite the fact he hates her. He is not going to let her go without a

fight. We worry that one day he is going to kill her. I worry what I

will do when I get the call that the evil beast has taken her from us

forever. My wild thoughts take control of my common sense. I can

see me killing his whole family. My anger knows no degree of stop.

She jokes that as soon as she was released from the prison

sentence the state gave her, she signed up for a life sentence with a

beast. I laugh with her all the while inside my heart is crying.

CHAPTER THREE

My mind is full of gambling thoughts. Normally, stress causes me to

see things that are not real. I hear voices. They do not always tell

me to do bad things. I can manage to do bad things all on my own.

The voices sometimes just cause confusion. I am sitting on this park bench with my legs propped up as if it were my couch. I am

watching a few winos beg other park goers for change. A few

mothers are pushing their children on the swings. No fathers in

sight. I was not fortunate like Jewel, I did not inherit a maternal

gene. I had my first daughter when I was eighteen, I named her

Rhiannon after the Stevie Nicks song. Her father did not stick

around to bounce names back and forth or offer any input

regarding her life whatsoever. I wanted to be a mother. I thought I

loved her before she even made her appearance in this world.

When she arrived, he vanished. My love for my child turned to

resentment. I loved him, and I begin to resent my baby because the

responsibility fell on me. I gave him my all and all he gave me was a

baby that neither of us could care for. He had the option of leaving.

I did not.

Each push the loving mothers give their cackling babies on the

swings sparks guilt in my heart. I wish I could have been like them

with my babies. Especially now. At least I would have someone to love me now. I was not even scaled as a somewhat decent mother.

Their dirty diapers gagged me. I would vomit at the putrid smells.

The other nastiness toddlers get into also made me sick to my tilt.

Babies require so much care, and I do not even care for my own self

well. The stress of their cries made my voices louder and way

worse. Back then mental illness was not everyday conversation.

When people spoke of the mentally ill they used terms like looney

bin, asylum and all of the places I dreaded to go if I had told

someone about what was really going on in my mind. I let my

babies lay in soaking wet and soiled diapers because I hated to go

through the effort of changing them. I would block out their

screams with a man or a good book. Just as easy as going to the

library for a book to check out is how nonchalantly, I continued my

search for affection from men. When one would leave, I would have

another before the next days sunrise.

I was getting attention while I should have been giving attention to

Rhiannon. We call her Rhi, or Rhi-rhi. Rhi, was taken by my oldest sister Polly. Also another amazing motherly role model that I have been exposed to in my life. Polly, is and has always been miss prim and proper. Things like cursing in public would make her blush. Fact is, Rhi, grew up with more than I ever could have provided her with. Polly, loved her like her own. Polly worked part time and steadfastly was a full time mother. Being young, childless and immature left me with a lot of free time on my hands. I ended up pregnant, again and again, and again. The next time I entered labor and delivery unit once again, I was alone. A bouncing baby boy. There was no crowd of family anxiously awaiting his arrival in the waiting room. His father was being sentenced to a first degree murder charge the day I went into labor. He was sentenced to life without the possibility o parole. It was a heinous crime. Necrophilia was involved. Jewel swears he is innocent, but I could careless. He denied my child the entire pregnancy so I will continue to deny his innocence. No daddy to snap horrible pictures and nobody there to hold my hands as intense labor pains sent hell through my body.

Truth is, my baby boy was not bouncing. He was clinging on to life.

Yes, I went to the bars while pregnant. But I never drank and I do

not smoke. I did not use drugs back then and was not under the

care of a psychiatrist. I ate, I exercised. Well actually I exercised only

by walking and looking for men. I count that. His tiny fist were

balled up as if he were a professional boxer. The nurses facial

expressions said the words before the doctors voice. He was not

supposed to make it. They wrapped him up as if he were already

dead and ran with him to NICU. No matter what they said I knew

the way his fist were tightly closed punching the world he was going

to make it.

I named him Champ. I do not remember the med flight to the

university hospital. I was sick too. I did not even notice how sick I

was. I just thought it was pregnancy and proceeded on with my

days.

Champ needed a pacemaker immediately. I was in the same

hospital but on a different wing. I was having radiation treatments five days a week, four hours a day. My parents, well the parents

that raised me were too old to drive that far to be by my bedside.

So they sent my second to the oldest sister Wava. She drove four

hours each way to aide us in the hospital.My hair fell out by the

clumps soon I was as bald as my baby, was there bringing me the

prettiest scarves you have ever laid your eyes on. For the first time

in my life I weighed less than one hundred fifty pounds. I spent a lot

of time reading the classics. The Adventures of Huckleberry Finn, To

Kill a Mockingbird, pretty much anything with paper and ink.

Thanksgiving brought a the city a massive snow storm. These Nor

Easterner storms sweep normal life task under snow piles. It makes

it impossible to get out in these temperatures and snow drifts. Of

course, I could not battle the storm anyway because I was still

hooked up like a science project. It was just another day of me

hooked up to wires. Just another day with me being pushed in a

wheelchair two floors and three hallways to visit my baby boy. I

had to be dressed in what seemed to be an astronaut training suit.

By the time the sun was blazing beams through my hospital room window, my bald head was growing peach fuzz. Champ, was fitting into newborn clothes. I wanted to be outside hanging out on the street corner with my friends. I did not to spend hours caring for a sickly baby. There I had a whole nursing staff plus Wava. When I went home I would be all alone with him. I just wanted a cool bandana to cover the patches of missing hair and a lot of sunshine.

By June, they were sending us home. My sister was overjoyed. She cared for Champ when I could not. She cared for me when I could not. To her we were like some plants she had watered from seeds and going home was blooming day. She could not wait to show us off. The first few days home I was exhausted from visits. Slowly, friends and family resumed back to their daily lives and I was left with too much time on my hands and a baby that still required too much care than I cared to give.

My father, passed away in July. We buried him and all of the motivation I ever had to change went in the ground with him. He would come clean my apartment for me. He did not want me to live in nastiness and especially have his grandchildren living in nasty. He was the only man that ever loved me. I pushed my parents love away because I wanted to be loved by some wild guy with long hair and a Harley, or just anyone who pretended to give a care about me. Daddy's death was dismissal for our entire family. He loved each of us whole heartedly but differently. No man will ever be born as great as he was.

When the tree branches lost their leaves and cool winds swirled through our days. Wava paced her clean floors worrying about us. I used Champ as leverage to get spending money from her and my brother in law. I would throw tantrums and not let them see Champ if she refused to give me money. It was not as if I was asking for a lot. Twenty to fifty bucks every weekend was more than enough. Wava, normally agreed to giving in because she knew that is what daddy would have wanted. Abruptly, she put a stop to all of that nonsense on Friday morning. Wava, sent her husband, Frank, to my door. I was entertaining company upstairs in my bedroom and

Champ was in the play pen in the living room crying. I heard

pounding on my door like the police or an angered wife. For a split

second my company thought perhaps I was married and I thought

the same about him. The banging did not stop. I haphazardly

wrapped a towel around me and galloped down the stairs. Frank

was standing there with a solemn look on his face. I blushed with

embarrassment.

"Muffy, Wava won't let me sleep. I am so terribly tired. I missed

work today in hopes I can resolve this and move on with our life.

She is my wife. I promised your dad when I married her no misery

will come her way as long as I can help it. She longer takes interest

in our life and marriage or our children. She spends all day, and

most of the night worrying about Champ. She is more focused on

what is going on in your house than what is going on in ours." He

took a deep breath and raised his head eye to eye with me. "Muffy,

I am here for Champ, so if you can gather his little things to get us

through the day we will be on our way." Just like that he thought he could waltz up to my door and take my baby. I was hesitating. I did not know what to say. "Muffy, I have a little money I will pay you whatever it takes. I can not afford what he is worth. I will pay you what I can. I have three thousand right now." I inhaled and shot him a wicked look. "Frank, I do not want your money, why didn't Wava come for him?" I asked in bewilderment. "Frank, I do not want any money for my baby. Y'all love him, y'all care for him better than I do or can. You can take him." I lifted Champ up with his wet diaper sagging and placed him into Franks arms.

No, I did not take a dime for him. My refrigerator looked new on the inside. I did not have money to fill it. I barely had enough for my daily Dr. Pepper fix. Since my daddy died I did not have anyone to go to the grocery store for me. But I did not feel as though it was right to take money from them. Because they were accepting my responsibility and giving him a second, third chance at life. I spun around on my heels and slid down the wall in tears. One more again I was childless. I knew it was the right thing to do, but my incompetence as a mother was still tugging on my heart strings. Slobbering cries, didn't take the pain away. The company I was entertaining could have cared less about my hurt. Men, like him only want you for the moment they don't want you for your problems. Frank, did wad up two hundred dollars and crush it in my hand as he was leaving. He told me that I could visit anytime. But he and I both knew that was highly unlikely.

CHAPTER FOUR

The sky is turning pink and the temperature has drastically dropped. I am lifting my heavy legs from the park bench. Leaving my guilt and my memories with my footprints and I keep stepping as if I am on a mission. Like someone who actually has a destination. I have a lot of family, but none that I want to call. I do not like staying in other peoples houses. I do not like feeling like a burden or out of place. I am starting to kick leaves and rocks to slower my pace as I continue to roam with no particular direction. I can not go home defeated to my mother. It is not like I do not want to see her. I would love too, she would love to see me too. She worries about me all day and prays for me all night. My brothers and sisters have banned me from my mothers. They say she is too old to deal with my irate behavior and sudden outburst of temper tantrums. We can talk on the phone, That is all we can do without causing turmoil amongst my mother and siblings. It is my choice to let them bully me away. I could go. It will be drama. That would upset her. So I keep my distance. None, of them could beat me in a fight. I subside and let them win.

The temperature keeps taking a drastic fall. One thing about living in the mountains is the temperature is about as stable as my address. You just never know when it will change. Up ahead I see a group of lost souls running from responsibilities like me. I speed up in hopes they will still be there when I get caught up to them. The rushing of my feet causes a slight stumble as I approach them. I invite myself to sit down beside of them. Ah… the joys of camaraderie. Nobody asks for my name. "You smoke?" The thin girl with the plaid shirt ask. "No." A guy wearing a wife beater with some misspelled tattoos and big eyes geekingly looks at me. "Are you a cop?" A nice looking guy with the prettiest blue eyes I have ever seen speaks up. "Shh, she isn't a cop, what cop have you ever seen wears wrinkles and expensive sandals. Plus she has a limp, cops cant have limps. Prevents them from chasing people." We all burst out in laughter. They continue to spark and pass, and skipping me. I step away while the two beside of me exhale. I do not want to breathe that stuff. "I like cocaine and punching people in the face. No other drugs do I dare touch." The crowd laughs again. I can literally get high just from the smoke. It has happened before and made my voices way worse. The girl wearing the red plaid shirt tied around her waist, breaks away from the group and flags down a gray sedan.

We all take turns shaking hands and introducing ourselves and carry on some witty banter. Yes it looks as if I have just stumbled upon my tribe. Darkness has fell on us. The nice looking guy, Sean, ask where do you live. I continue to explain why my answer is nowhere. He shoots me a sly smile. "You can come with me to the fellowship home. They take in everyone." I am uneasy about going to a strange place. Sean reassures me that I will be welcomed there. "I wont steer you wrong." He says. I still go against my better judgement and follow him to the three story house across the street. There is no grass growing in the yard. I hear the words that float through my mind in my aunt Myras voice. "Devils lurk, in houses who have no grass.. just dirt." I continue up the porch steps paying little attention to the cobwebs on the steps. A couple of shutters are missing pieces or not hanging at all. Sean turns the door knob and steps aside to let me in. It is rare in life that a man has ever opened the door for me.

A slender lady walks from the kitchen. Her face tells a story of many miles on a motorcycle traveling with a brotherhood of drug dealers and addicts, wild bonfires and no parental guidance from an early age. Much to my surprise, she speaks with eloquence. I am slightly intimidated by how well spoken her short words are. "You are welcome, to stay here, if you wish. Do not confuse my hospitality with ignorance. In the morning someone will go over a list of rules for you to abide by. I do not live here, but this is my home away from home." She smiled and returned back to the kitchen table working through her paperwork. Feeling somewhat dumbfounded I hang my hand and glance at the hardwood floors that needs refinished. I just went from nowhere to stay to somewhere to stay. I went from carrying around loneliness to being in the midst of a house full of people.

Full ashtrays decorate the end tables beside of the couch and recliner. The Holy Bible and the Holy grail of AA books sit in the center of the coffee table. It is not inviting like a grandmothers house here. The donations of odds and ends furniture show comfort but nothing shows a home here. A petite older lady with a raspy voice leads me upstairs. Her voice sounds like she made a living pumping gas and smoking non filter camels. If alcoholism were a person she would be listed. Her sentences are slow as if she has suffered some kind of traumatic brain injury or perhaps she has wet brain. She explains women sleep on this floor and men sleep on the third level of the house. We are not allowed to lay up with our boyfriends here. The paneling on the walls dims the room. I am too exhausted to worry about checking for bed bugs or roaches. I am mentally spun and I just want to rest so that I can figure out my next move.

My last conscious thought was wondering who laid in this bed before me? What kind of diseases did they carry? Did they leave? Who all in this house shared that disease? Did they find it here or just leave it? What if I am overthinking? This soft warm bed invites to drift further and further into sleep. The Goldilocks in me, submits to my dreams instead of my anxiety. I am awakened by the smell of hash browns. I slightly open my eyes. Vaguely I hear Sean rattling a bag. I thought men were not allowed to be in female rooms. I am

still half asleep and I fight to open both eyes widely. Yes, I want

hash browns. This bed is so comfortable. It has been two years

since I have slept on a real mattress. I fight to sleep while fighting to

wake up. I feel the touch of his soft hand grabbing mine. I reach for

my glasses. That is a sign that waking up won the fight. He is

bringing me breakfast in bed. He hands me a cup of ice cold Dr.

Pepper. How does he know that is my drink? McDonald's. But it is

still breakfast in bed. I have never had anyone bring me anything

much less to the bed.

I was raised in an immaculately clean home. My mother cleaned

even when it was not dirty. Our carpets never showed years of wear

and tear only vacuum streaks. Yet, I manage to sleep well in the

slums. I inhale the McDonald's. I pay no attention to his cuteness or

his charm as I gulp down the Dr.Pepper. Most men are never

around when I wake up. To think we did not even sleep together.

He just may be Mr.Right, or at least Mr.Right now. His sparkling blue eyes refreshes my soul already. We spend the next few minutes with meaningless chit chat and he kisses me on the forehead before he leaves. I am blushing in places I have never felt blush. A true gentleman. He mentioned he admired my minimalistic point of views. I do not care for things that other woman tend to care about. Appearance, being the first. Materialistic views. If it was meant for me to have it, I would have it so I just leave it at that. Painted shiny nail and make-up I would not have a clue how to begin in those areas. My nails are brittle often times bitten so far down in the quick I feel the tips throbs when I touch things. Uneasily, I walk downstairs. I am nervous about seeing people that I do not know. I feel outcasted until a tall, slim, and eloquent speaking lady approaches me. She hands me a list of house rules. I read each rule and study my surroundings. I observe the rules I am reading must be laxed.

Rule number three, I have already broken. No men in rooms where females sleep. A formal introduction. "I am Barbara, nobody calls me that. Babs, is what everyone calls me." She smiles and I tell her

"My name is Muffy." Babs smiles at my silly nickname. She sits at the table and offers me coffee. I decline the coffee but accept the invite to sit down. Sure Enough! I was right to judge a book by the cover. This hippie chick let the behaviors of the sixties go strong in her life until the mid-eighties. At some point in life Babs, thought herion and Harleys were more exciting than her exams in college. She told me how she traded the university education in for the school of hard knocks. She spoke about riding with motorcycle gangs across the country. Her skin tone and wrinkles display the truth behind her awesome stories.

Just like me, Babs grew up with a white picket fence and house to match. Babs, got clean and married a recovered cocaine addict. Now they both dedicate their life to saving lost souls like mine. I have often heard about overcoming love stories such as theirs the AA meetings are full of inspiring people with stories that mimic theirs. Unfortunately, I have never known them to remain successful in the addiction battle. Babs, has to be strong minded. I heard coming off that junk was hell on earth and you had to be tough as nails to endure the withdrawals. My addiction, is not, nor was it ever alcohol. The party is my drug of choice. The attention, the watching the ones wilder than me, the competition to be wilder than them. That is what I thrive on. My crazy tends to be hidden a little better on the bar scene than it does in the other norms of society. The little hand is even with the big hand on the clock. This morning has buzzed by. Sean, returns in and I can not help but to feel the same blush I felt this morning on his sight.

He has not retuned in the same condition he left in. His beautiful blue eyes are now glassy and droopy. His speech slurred. His balance is off as if he is suffering from Parkinson's disease. My nervous energy is gravitating to panic mode. What if Babs, comes back in and puts up both out of this cozy spot? He is posing too much of a risk. I take a seat on the couch and strike up a rambling conversation with a tall skinny lady who is smoking a cigarette. Her smoke is choking me and making my head hurt. I continue to ramble keeping my mind and attention off of Sean. The whole room

of five people are staring at him. Yet, not one of them except me

seems surprised. This must be a common state for him. He staggers

over to where I am sitting. In my mid-sentence he collapses into my

lap.

He is not dead or at least I do not think he is. He might be? I have

never experienced someone pass out on my lap so I am unsure as

what to do. Everyone is continuing there conversation, except for

Frankie, he is laughing hysterically at Sean and my surprise.

"Kamikaze" he cackles even louder. He mimics the fall while holding

his jiggling stomach. Sean, is unbothered by my nudges no matter

how hard I nudge. He continues to slobber on my lap and snore

even louder. Traci, clears up my confusion as she walks past and

says. "XANAX." I am naïve. I only know about alcohol and cocaine.

All of this other exposure is all new to me. I did not realize you

could get that high on Xanax. I remember when it was prescribed to

me but I do not like pills especially their side effects. When I got evicted full bottles of anti-psych drugs filled my medicine cabinet in the bathroom.

His resting face weighs heavy on my thighs while the thoughts of my past weigh heavy on my mind. He sleeps so peaceful on me. I count the perfections in his bone structure and continue on with my rambling chatter. I look down at his strong jaw bone and high cheekbones. This could be the start of a special romance. He is comfortable enough to pass out on my and I am comfortable enough to eat in front of him. Traci, breaks my concentration by passing around a picture of her three children she finally gets a visitation right to this coming weekend.

I gaze her blonde hair chubby cheeked blue eyed children. I wonder what my children are doing. Most of the time I block them out so I do not wallow in guilt. I know they are well taken care of. I know first hand the kind of love my older sisters gave me so I know without a shadow of doubt they love my children more than life itself. I also rely on the fact, my kids are raised as cousins not

siblings and they are far better off with the families they have now,

instead of me. I lack the ability to differentiate the difference

between love and sex. One of the consequences to that is my third

and final child will never know what genetic traits her DNA is made

up of. Once more, I found myself alone and stuck with a squalling

baby. I would bounce around from house to house so that others

could care for my baby while I slept or partied on the weekends.

CHAPTER FIVE

Ella-Mae was born in the spring. Ella-Mae my mothers namesake.

Mom, hated that I gave my baby her name. She always hated that

name. Alisha came and helped me tremendously with her. She kept

her for days at a time. I would drop off a dirty, sticky baby and pick

up a bouncing happy clean baby. Often times, I thought I should just

leave her there and not return but I loved Alisha so much I did not want to terminate our friendship. Alisha, was not financially apt to care for a another child. She already had her own five year old. Winter blew us high snows that measured in feet not inches. It made it unbearable to get out and couch hop. I stayed trapped in my tiny apartment with my baby, longing for company.

I busy myself with reading to keep my mind off of my life. I tend to spend hours at times wondering what I have done in life to deserve this kind of loneliness. I have always gave my all to my relationships only to end up single mothered again. The poorly insulated windows, made that apartment draft in cold air. I keep a blanket on the couch to snuggle up with. I would have rather be accompanied by a man, any man. Even, one that in Sabras words "was not even worth the gun powder to blow him to hell." That is her infamous line to describe men who are not fit for breathing and too sorry for dying.

Most days I feel like a mattress with a hole in it. Defective, yet still useful. I am uncomfortable in my own skin. I listened to the advice of others. Who told me, "Clean your apartment you will feel better." They disregard the fact I needed to feel better to be able to clean. I listened when they told me, "Get up, fix breakfast, it is the most important part of the day." I lack the ability or skill to know how to cook. When I try, I only disappoint my taste buds. A Tijuana Mama and a Dr. Pepper, chip and dip. That is my normal dietary way to start the day.

The colder that apartment got the lonelier, it became. The rain would leave moisture on the sills of the windows. Even if I had of kept it clean. It still would have a musty smell. Death seemed to surround everywhere I ever lived. When I was raising Rhiannon, one Friday night I happened to be home with her which was a rarity. The neighbor to the adjoining apartment provided her best friend a safe haven to hide from her abusive husband. That is the night I learned evil was real. I heard a deafening boom, then another one and another one. Shots rang out blowing holes in my walls. If Rhi

and I would have been sleeping we would have lost our lives that

night too. I used to see that lady at the bars and in passing on our

way in and out of our apartments. She was picture perfect. She had

the face of Delta Burke and the body of Farrah Faucet. What kind of

man would do that to her. That sawed off shot gun blew Mrs. Sara

into two pieces.

Again, death would lurk close to me in the Shimmies. This time

there was no rhyme nor reason. A body rolled up in a blanket was

discovered. If I had of paid more attention or washed more dishes. I

easily could have noticed the blanket in eye shot of my kitchen

window. As thirty police cars lights casted blue lights in the night

sky. I thought "Wow, how cruel, to throw a human a way like

yesterday's garbage. I will not lie, for a few minutes I wished that it

was me out there laying with deer feeding off of my body. In the old

green quilt, was the body of an eighteen year old woman. She did not even have a chance in life to do any wrong to anyone, yet her life had been taken.

I guessed they tossed her out there by the tracks assuming by the looks of our building it must have been vacant. The railroad engineer happen to notice a foot sticking out of the blanket. Later, on we would find out that little girl had died at the hands of her fifty seven year old sugar daddy. I have never experienced being loved to death. I had wondered what that was like. As I watched them lift that tiny girl onto the stretcher, I wondered if he showed her mercy or did he cause her excruciating pain. I was close enough to see too much but still far enough away not to be able to determine what possibly had happened to cause her death. That was somebody's daughter being bagged and tagged. I wondered if they had loosened their parental bonds and turned her out for the streets to tear apart. Or if she had been a runaway unknowingly sealing her fate.

Trapped with a crying child, I filled her bottles with soda or whatever I could find to soothe her cries. Some days that worked and some days it did not. Her loud screams and total isolation made the recipe for my voices to get worse. I never looked into my baby's eyes and felt a sense of pride for bringing such a beautiful creature into this world. All, I ever saw was, MISERY. I named her after the greatest woman and impact in my life, yet I found no joy. Her diaper sagged as she crawled on her knees. I did not have a clue as to what to do to soothe the floor marks on her knees. Maggots danced through old pizza boxes I was too lazy to toss in the trash. Actually my trash bags were already overflowing. My apartment was filled with the rancid scent of dirty clothes and soiled diapers. I would open my door to wayward couples who for whatever reason had no place to stay during the storms.

In exchange for a dry bed, they would clean my apartment and care for Ella-Mae while I slept or took a walk in the blizzard. When the snows melted, they would find a reason to leave, and make it on their own. By the time the apartment gathered its usual filth a different friend may need housed. There is only so many struggling people a person knows. When I ran out of people who needed me. The apartment got over taken with flies, roaches and maggots. I had no choice but to move. I was evicted the first time the landlord came in for a cleaning inspection. Clothes on my back and a empty diaper bag and Ella Mae on my hip. I jumped into my aunt Myras car and never looked back on that apartment again. My aunt Myra, would give you the shirt off of her back. Her heart was more generous than her finances would allow. Her loving heart was masked by cigarette smoke and colorful curse words. If she was breathing you better believe she was cussing something or somebody. She may have spoke harsh words, maybe she needed to. Every night at her house was a slumber party. We were grown women with children giggling over bar gossip or silly tv shows. She would cook the best meals and we floated like teenagers. She took excellent care of Ella-Mae. Matter of fact Ella- Mae reached for her before she would reach for me. And her first words was MY-MY.

Jewel, is my aunt Myras oldest daughter. Me and Jewel would

concoct plans on how to get free restaurant food. In our minds we

were helping Myra out so that she did not have to cook. Myra,

never seemed to notice or care that our pockets stayed broke yet

we always had money for restaurant food. Until, one day three

employees tried to chase us down because we dined and ditched at

the Mexican restaurant. Best fajitas I have ever ate to this day. It

was the thrill. I thought she was going to beat us to death when she

looked through the rear view and heard three men chasing us and,

screaming in broken English.

She would cuss me out daily, mostly because I sucked as a mother. I

lacked the motivation to pick up after myself. Back talking her was

never an option for me. She was right with every swear word she

tossed at me and her reputation gave founded reason that if I were

to cuss her back there was a great possibility she would take a

butcher knife to me. She would most likely do it with as much ease as picking my damp towels off of the bed. Months passed before I wore out my welcome. She got attached to Ella-Mae, so that afforded me the ability to stay longer than she wanted me to. Endlessly, she drove me around so I could find a place to live.

Before, I got the keys to the apartment, mom made Frank purchase me a low grade dependable car. A Snow White Pontiac Bonneville. It ran like a dream, and I never cared about the date on the car, as long as it got me from point a to point b. Mom, had hopes that if I had a car I would enter into the workforce. I was not ready for that kind of commitment to life. I accepted the car anyway. My brothers and sisters gossiped their opinions about how they felt that I was going to break mom and she would not have money to last the duration of her lifetime if she kept giving to me. I hustled daily needs by giving people rides places and charging them gas or fast food for my services. I still received my government assistance and the apartment was approved for HUD. I could live off of the bare minimum, so I did.

I found an apartment on the edge of a curve down a winding country road. Behind the apartment building just a few feet away was some very active railroad tracks. The building was held together with white cinderblocks. The windows were paper thin. I think plexiglass would have been better insulated that the glass squares. My new address was called the Shimmeys because every time the train passed it rattled the glass. From the front door, you could see every room in the house including the back door. Sometimes the trains rolled through so fiercely it would shake the foundation. That would upset, Ella Mae and she would scream to the top of her lungs. That would cause the voices to etch into my mind like nails on a chalkboard. It would take hours to settle down. Of all the days and nights I spent watching how Myra cared for my baby and cooking and cleaning, I did not leave her house with not one of those skills. I never even tried. The task was too overwhelming.

I learned not only were my voices not to be trusted but people could not be trusted. During a lengthy phone conversation and the need to let some weight escape from my heart I confided in my dear friend, Piper about a night I had experienced. Piper and me had a developing friendship since I was carrying Ella-Mae. We met on the bar scene. We dated brothers and our friendship out lasted both of those relationships. Wind whistled in the trees, and I could not distinguish if the leaves rattling were just the wind, or a demonic entity. I was as sober as a judge, yet I still could not make sense of anything on that frigidly cold September night. The trained rolled down the track at full throttle evoking a scream from Ella-Mae, I couldn't soothe. The demons in my mind would not subside. I palmed my ears to no avail. I just wanted them to shut up. I just wanted my baby to shut up. I was consumed with confusion and noise. My legs began to feel heavy as if I were walking against the oceans ebb.

I secured Ella-Mae, in her car seat. As the words in my mind instructed me to do. I lifted the car seat off of the floor and carried her the short distance to the train tracks. The cold fogged my glasses as I breathed a fog of water vapor. I noticed a look of fear on Ella-Maes apple shaped face. I kept stepping. I walked her out about fifty yards from the building and left her in the middle of the tracks. She was quiet on my walk back so that confirmed I was doing the right thing. I returned inside and kicked my shoes off embracing the feeling of peace and relaxation. It was almost euphoric. The quietness. I got a sudden burst of energy and for the first time in my life I actually wanted to wash dishes. I looked out of the kitchen window in blackness of the dark night. I scraped old left over food into the trash. I went back to the sink and gazed out to the pitch black air. Then it hit me like a tons of bricks. My baby girl was out there. If that train comes back through there is never no way I can explain how she got outside secured in the car seat.

My feet fumbled underneath each other as I ran as fast as I could going to retrieve my baby girl. Her cherub face was reddened with the cold. Her soft skin felt moist with coldness. I had not intended on killing my child. I got her back to the living room floor and unzipped her coat as soon as the train rumbled by shimmying the windows once more. That time Ella-Mae, did not make a sound. The fear was still framed around her cherub face. Perhaps even as an infant she possessed a survival of the fittest mentality. Piper, repeated my mishap to child protective services. Which brought forth me a new battle to fight.

My extensive vocabulary impressed the slightly educated case worker. I denied the accusations of such an outlandish story. She whole heartedly bought my lie, but due to the way my apartment looked when she came she opened a case anyway. She was young and still believed she could change the world with her kind acts towards humanity. I nurtured her naïve sense and she really looked forward to coming by my house. She found me another apartment, a two bed room in an apartment complex on a hillside. She worked diligently until she succeeded in expediting a section 8 voucher so that I could afford to live in the complex. Mom, worked on having her old living room and bedroom suites hauled to my new apartment.

That was supposed to be my new beginning restart number five. A car, an affordable decent housing. The CPS worker got me into a mental health doctor and my real problems began shortly there after. I was honest with the questionnaire. I was honest when I sat down in the dimly lit doctors office and spoke in depth with the Syrian doctor. He nodded his head and jotted down notes. Before my exit he handed me a stack of prescriptions. The child protective service worker said it was part of my safety plan that I take all prescribed medications. So I did. I complied without hesitation on every thing she asked. Except the cleaning. The concoctions of anti psych drugs did silence the voices in my head. They also, silenced my drive to get out of bed. I was lethargic and numb to the world around me. Ella-Mae still cried, but with the medicine I could ignore her cries. Life still threw curve balls but I was too tired to dodge them. I took them as needed as prescribed, and as forced by a social worker who trusted the mental health system.

My mothers hand me down furniture eventually looked like it was handed down from a dumpster instead of the cleanest house in the world. The sweet worker, took that as if I needed a parenting class, and to learn cleaning skills. So on each Thursday at 2pm sharp. I had a mentor coach to teach me how to properly tend to my house work. Also, a parenting coach. I hated Thursdays more than any other day. After four solid months of Thursday intrusions, they deemed me uninterested in the betterment of our life. A decision had to be made. Would Ella-Mae, live with Myra or would she go to foster care permanently or would she go to my quadriplegic brother, Will, and his nurse wife. Unfit and incompetent I was about to be childless once more.

I understood it was for the best. Will and his wife stepped up and before the week was over they were parents. Will has an IQ that qualified him for Mensa. He never allowed his disability to hinder his ability to work. He was paralyzed from the neck down in a swimming accident shortly after his nineteenth birthday. Mom, acted as his nurse, caregiver, best friend and mother his whole adult life. Will worked as a director of operations for a nursing home funded by the state. That is how he was able to met his nurse wife. His paralysis did not stop his handsome face from shining through his adversities. Belle seemed to have loved him very much and could have cared less he had to sign their marriage license with a pen in his mouth not in his hand. They bought a cottage style house in the country. Ella- Mae would have a big yard to explore once she learned to walk. She would learn to be the smartest girl in the whole school with those two teaching her. She would grow up to have a work ethic which I lacked. Or so I had hoped. The remnants of my short temper would no longer bruise and scar my baby. She was adored.

Once more I had became childless. Once more I had failed as a parent. No more merrily maids coming to rescue me from my filthy apartment every Thursday. No need to continue taking that horrible variety of medicines. My five dollar words would be replaced with my foul bar mouth. Piper, eventually plead her case, I thanked her for her concern and understood and forgave her with my whole heart. We became the best of the bar flies. The trust would be rebuilt through our preceding escapades. Alisha and Myra had their hearts ripped out when they realized they may never lay eyes on Ella-Mae again. It was truly for the best for all involved.

CHAPTER SIX

All good things must come to an end. Our time at the fellowship home was up. Seans constantly being high and us constantly being seen in each other's rooms was obvious disrespect for the household rules. We were kindly ordered to leave by the end of the week. We were not completely kicked out. Abiding by rules is something I have always struggled with. It truly has nothing to do with lack of respect, but everything to do with lack of regard for consequences. Seams, mother could not bare to see her only child out in the cold. One sobbing "Mama, please help me and I won't ever ask for another dime" cry was enough to land us the deposit for an apartment. Of course, throughout out relationship that same cry was a weekly thing, and rewarded weekly each time she believed her son was going to snap away from whatever demons kept him down. Our apartment was nice and came furnished. I figured since Seans mother had paid for us an apartment, my mother could help us too.

It was my turn to shoot my shot at one more "Mama, please help me I will never ask you for another dime." Cry. Success was achieved and mom went and co-signed for me a brand spanking new Ford Escort. He stayed high on Xanax. With each days passing he could take an additional ten more than the previous day. He was delightful when not high but those times were far and few between. He would hustle his mother for money to make the car payment and whatever else he could hustle went on pills. Sean, would get arrested for foolishness and sometimes felonies. All nonviolent, but finally he was out of chances and he got sentenced to prison. I visited the jail a few times but never like a devoted girlfriend should. I would write him letters and forget to put them in the mail. I spent most of my weekends with Piper.

Pipers, new husband was charming. He was not very attractive but he was a good provider and stayed in great spirits. He appeared to be a wonderful family man. Almost heroic for standing up as a step father to her eldest son. Fishing and camping trips. Money for pizza the fun never seemed to ceased. He loved Piper, not her eldest son. He could not make himself love him and when Roger got drunk. The eldest boy took the brunt of the booze. Piper, always made excuses for Roger saying that he had to teach the boy discipline. Roger, never worked a day in his life at at what society calls a real job. Roger was a good ole boy rebel flag waving poor grammar having hustler. His book sense may have been lacking but he knew more about the law than the legislature. He also knew math, quite well. Fractions and chemistry. Roger is what the police would and eventually did consider a king pin. Throughout their marriage Piper gave birth two more times. Roger, never made nobody question he had his kids and she had hers. I realize I have no room to judge anyone on love or parenting. I was not raised like that. If you married the mom you married her kids. Everyone I had ever met up until that point shared my same belief system.

He did not purchase cocaine in baggies. His supplies came in bricks. Having that kind of quantity and quality makes you a local celebrity. A feared outlaw. He would babysit the boys while me and Piper would hit the bars. One night he sent us with 3.5 grams of powder to the bar. "If y'all take this y'all wont have to pay for one drink."

Out of curiosity Piper and me grabbed a straw and sniffed what we thought was going to be some kind of euphoric magic. It was not. Maybe we did it wrong the first time? We took that bag and did as he instructed. He was right, we did not pay a dime for anything. We were the belles of the bar. It brought us joy to see everyone enjoy what we hated. So the following Friday night, there we were supplying free cocaine to everyone redneck while they supplied us top shelf bourbon. One in particular Friday night we followed Sheila in the lady's room. She creased a dollar bill down the center and Piper loaded it up for her. Piper nor I were familiar with the amounts and math. Piper just sprinkled. Sheila was impressed with Pipers generosity. Sheila sniffed across the bill like an aardvark.

Sheila passed the bill back to Piper then Piper went across the bill, then she passed it to me and I followed suit. We were blitzed at that point. We were incapable of making decisions. That was a bad one. That time we found the shocking euphoria. That time our face went numb. Our brains did as well. I was seduced by the rush. For the first time in my entire life I was fully at peace. I was aware of my

surroundings, yet I could not participate in the chaos, nor did I want

to. It was a moment of clarity. We found the euphoria. We

embraced it. Every weekend became a moment of clarity. Soon,

those weekends with cocaine turned into weekdays with it. Roger,

did not care how much we were doing. The more Roger, would sell

the less he would drink. He stayed high as well. I believe he got his

rush from the power and the notoriety. Our time for clarity

transpired from the bar to hanging out daily and playing scrabble or

going shopping.

I stopped making car payments because I no longer had money. Any

spare money I had I bought more cocaine. I still had no job. The

bank started harassing mom for the car payments. That really

infuriated her. Her credit score was valuable to her. I was in the

process of ruining it. It was just a credit score, but she acted as if it

were her kidney or some major organ. So Mom, had me meet her at

the bank. She wrote a check for eleven thousand dollars. I had only ever heard my mom curse twice in life. Both times I was at fault. "This doesn't make any damn sense Muffy, this is your inheritance. When I die all of my other children will get a check but you will not get anything." Who cared I did not. Who really imagines that one day their mom is going to die. I sure did not. Mom, has always tried her very best with all she knew to do with me. It is like the old saying goes, I am the only hell my mama ever raised.

Eventually, life lead me to another friend that just happened to love to escape from her low self esteem. Cassandra, was not overweight like me. She was morbidly obese. She was the exact opposite of the physical description of a drug user. Cassandra, affectionately known as Sandy hustled even when she had money. She was a pioneer of boosting from stores. She was pushing televisions out of Walmart before stores needed spider wrap sensors to guard their merchandise from people like her. Cassandra was so large she could conceal microwaves, and other small appliances under her shirt. A person can only sell small stolen appliances for so long in a scarcely populated area. When that side business, halted at times.

Cassandra would have me drive her around while she lifted

neglected purses from shopping carts, even doctors offices. One

time even a gas station attendant. She would spend those credit

cards and write those checks like they had her name on them. It is

the little things that get you caught. One day she was arrested for

shoplifting. The police went through her purse and found fifteen

cards with fifteen different names. I was shortly indicted on

conspiracy to commit a felony. Which is how, I came about

becoming an inmate.

I hated the cold drabness of that place. I adapted to it because I had

to. There is not much choice in the matter. It is obnoxiously loud.

The smell was worse than any apartment I have ever dirtied up.

Musty, mold scents flavor ever meal, and snack. Women more

mentally ill than me, overcrowded the system. I did not participate

in the sweaty workout sessions that the state allowed us to have for

recreation. Something about the bars on the windows made it lose the Golds Gym theme they were spending funding on. I would watch those women with natural life sentences sweat until they looked drowned and think to myself, why do they go through all of this for a healthy fit body to live in here longer. I suppose hopes of appeals is what kept them jumping.

There was no Dr. Pepper in there. It was Coke or Pepsi or water. I guzzled the Coke, but I was not happy to do it. Sundries of women, whose failures resulted in them giving the state, the time that was supposed to go to their families. Their children. I belonged to an elite class there. The smart ones. The ones who could read and comprehend. Paralegals, teachers, insurance representatives and nurses who stole more drugs from their employers than they administered to their patients. We were the lucky ones. We could read a book to escape the confinement of the cinderblock and razor wire chain linked fencing that surrounded us. There were some women, who could not even read or understand their sentencing orders.

The scales of the judicial system seemed to me to be unbalanced. Women who were impoverished had more lengthy sentences of lesser crimes than those who had families to flip the bill for their legal expenses. I did not feel as if I deserved to be living in those conditions. I felt jilted. I realize I committed a crime. Although at the time I was driving and being rewarded in the benefits Cassandra stole, I did not know I was committing a crime. The judge who handed down my sentence said "Ignorance of the law is no excuse." In comparison my crime was not even worth wasting the time of the circuit court. My cell block was full of women who had done the most heinous things imaginable. Baby killing, child molesting, murdering for thrill killing. There I was, with a handful of a few drug dealers, addicts and embezzlers were mingled in with them. It did not seem fair. The thing that kept me going was I knew I was only there for a temporary moment of time. No matter our differences were we as unit of a tribe there

I got along with all of those women once I figured that out. I only had dramatics with Cassandra. I felt she was responsible for me being there. I took my anger out on her every chance I got. Especially when I saw she had made more friends there than I did. That was partly because the revered queen CeeCee took a likening to her. CeeCee, thought she should be respected because she had to serve life with the possibility of parole. In her days of freedom she was a drug dealer. Some kid, a seventeen year old boy owed her fifteen dollars. When he could not pay. She shot him in his face, killing him instantly. Some kind of way an unwritten prison code said that I should respect her. I did not abide by that. I thought that was the dumbest story I had ever heard and when I said to her. "Why did you not, just ask someone else to loan you the fifteen dollars? It seems to me, as a drug proprietor you should have had at least fifteen dollars and not need to kill anyone, especially a child for it?" Cee Cee took great offense to my comment. I was not there to make friends I was there to serve time.

I wondered what kind of environment CeeCee grew up in the city of Detroit. How she had fled from her gangland streets to the mountains. It is possible she could not earn respect in her birthplace so, she fled to make money and a name for herself elsewhere. Unsuccessful with respect in the mountains as well. She must have thought earning respect from a bunch of women inmates would have to suffice. I wondered if her mental illness gave her symptoms of a feeling of grandeur and if her parents had ever taught her anything.

I had good parents because I was adopted by my paternal grandparents. That is why Wava, and them are so much older than me. I am not only a late in life child I was the baby of the bunch. Everyone's shining pride. Our white home with the slate blue shutters had scandals like everyone else. We were just not allowed to mention them at the dinner table or no other table for that matter. Dad, worked his back out in the coal mines. He certainly was not always a God-fearing man. He was a weekend bar hopping gambling gun toting rumored to be a card carrying member of the Klu Klux Klan. All that life would be left behind come Sunday mornings when my Bible toting bake selling church fundraising mother needed him in the pew beside of her. He never missed a Sunday even though he had not been saved until the last seven years of his life. Mom, never spoke nor fussed with him about his weekend adventures. There were never no illustrious affair rumors around town circling his name so Mom did not care what he was doing. He liked to drink and gamble. Gambling or drinking were not welcome into my mothers home. She would not bend the rule even for the man that crippled his body buying her a house.

By the time I was sixteen I was already tainted with sin. I loved every second of it. No more was I being bullied, I became the bully. Dad, spoiled me and saw no wrong in anything I could do. Mom however was growing tired of wretching her hands and wearing her knees out praying for me. She asked God for guidance, but I was being led by the devil. She asked the Lord for patience but I tested the limit. So one sunny afternoon, she demanded that I get out of bed. Of course I cussed her out because I was offended she had awakened me before 3pm. I stomped through the house like a spoiled six year old disappointed on Christmas. Mom, already had the car door open. I did not want to go anywhere. She drug me kicking and screaming the whole way. I had no clue where she was taking me but I knew I did not want to go. She slammed me in the backseat like she was a hostile police officer hauling a belligerent drunk to jail. She drove me to my biological mothers apartment in the projects! I was mortified. Mom, barely slowed downed she demanded that I "GET OUT NOW!" Her newfound aggression was something I had never been the brunt of. I was scared that I finally had pushed her too far. I did as I was told.

Sitting high on the hillside was a face that looked just like mine. I knew where I was and why she dropped me off like a stray dog with mange. She sent me home. The face like mine was sitting amongst her neighbors on a wooden picnic table. I knew the bleach blonde plump lady with the Rod Stewart spiked haircut had to be who I was

sent to. I could not get over how her facial features were a mirror

image to mine. She had a few more wrinkles than me. She knew

right away who I was and why I was there. A group of obnoxious

teenagers were congregating, a few yards away. My eyes were

fixated on the tall blonde guy. He had bright blue eyes just like

mine, although we had zero resemblance. His eyes confirmed we

shared the same DNA. Butterflies danced about in my stomach. I

had hoped my mother would jump up from the table and run to

hug me. I envisioned a lifetime movie re-enactment. I braced myself

for a sobbing hug that only the jaws of life could pry apart. Which

by the way to this very day I am still waiting on.

She never rose to her feet. Her words stung like a thousand bees.

"She wanted you, she got you, she needs to be the one to finish

raising you." She saw my eyes start to water up and she got up from

the table and barely hugged my shoulder. It was more like the kind

of hug a funeral director gives you when they finish taking all of your money. Not the embrace I had longed for. "Go on inside and tell that old hag to come back and pick you up." I raised my eyebrows and braced my feet for a fight "No." Sabra, said "I am not some white trash they lead you to believe I am!" "Oh no I only found out I was adopted this past Thursday and by the looks of things I was very lucky." Sabra, yelled "Allison, come down here." She had to call Allisons name three times before the palest most beautiful girl I ever laid my eyes on pounced through the yard as if she were part giraffe with long strides. She snatched me up in her arms and gave me the hug Sabra was supposed to give me. She held on to me as if she were missing something precious and finally found it. "Take Muffy, inside and let her call her mother to come back and get her." Allison snapped back, "You are her mother! I finally have a sister, a real sister." She begged our mother to let me stay as if I were a lost puppy with a cute face. Sabra, finally shook her head and submitted. She squinted her eyes and gazed me over as if she were intending on finding any tiny flaws. Her microscopic squints made me uneasy. "You must be wild and that must be why she sent you here. Yeah, that has got to be it. That hateful hag would not have never returned you to me if something were not wrong with you." I was offended and flabbergasted she would refer to my God-fearing mother in such a way.

Soon, I was introduced to that tall blonde boy. I did not care about his young life choices, none of that mattered to me. He was my brother, that is all that mattered. One by one I would get to really know his friends. Seemed like that group was more like one. They stood in unity. It was obvious they all were more than friends. They were the same brain working in different bodies. That totally embarrassed him because he was not overprotective like my other brothers. My promiscuity embarrassed him amongst his low life train jumping weed smoking school skipping friends. From that early on their decisions plagued their futures and their destiny was determined. Short turmoil filled lives. Sabra, was impoverished to say the least. Four cinderblocks held up her couch. No chairs sitting underneath the kitchen table. I had heard about how the poor lived but I never imagined it was that minimal. Sabra, sit with elderly

people in the daylight hours five days a week. As soon as she would

get off of her day job she would start her mid evening hustle.

Sabra, Allison and me would pile into burgundy Mercury Zephyr

that had been gifted to her from her mother Stevie, as she drove

around bootlegging the commodity cheese to bar owners and

restaurant owners. Still to this day bulk cheese makes me smile.

Sabra, would tell me stories about my biological father. Mom, never

spoke a word of his name. He disappeared and from then on she

did not even have a picture of him in the home. Her own son. When

they adopted me, they disowned him. Sabra, told me all about their

fairytale wedding. I gained a sense of my background. Digging up

memories for her made me grounded to my present. Sabra, said

their love was one for the story books but did admit she found him

somewhat boring because he loved to read and she loved to dance.

Sabra, told how he lived his life to appease others. Clearly, from her

demeanor she was a free spirit who could care less of the opinions of others. "He was outright ashamed of you, Muffy. He did not want no crippled baby, you were too heavy for me to carry by myself. I did not have this weight on me then. I was 36" 26" 36" I had hips but they were not strong enough to bare the weight of those hunks of metal draping across your legs." She went to say that all they did was argue about who was going to carry me. He insisted that I lay in the crib with the door shut when company came over. He acted as if you were severely physically deformed. And would have preferred "a bullet to his brain than to be seen with you."

Later on in the evening Sabra would disappear into the night. She claimed she was working as a bar tender four nights a week. I was having the time of my life sitting on that couch held up by cinderblocks. Remnants of brutal fights between Allison and Scooter splattered on the walls and ceiling. Nobody but me ever questioned why there was macaroni noodles dried by the light on the kitchen ceiling. You name it, those two went to war over it. I really felt at peace in the midst of the chaos. Nobody here held nothing back. Eventually, I got comfortable enough to jump in from time to time and help Allison get the best of him. Gone were the days he could stand on her head while he friends cheered him on and dared her to move. Allison was my baby sister, I defended her. I had to. I would grab a knife or hammer, just anything I could wield at him to cease the violence. I often wondered what horrendous acts Scooters friends felt comfortable doing to my baby sister when nobody was around to have her back. I did not partake in the cigarette or weed smoking. Only the fighting. What is chaos to the fly is bliss to the spider. I found my place of where my spirit had belonged.

CHAPTER SEVEN

A whole two months went by wit me living the rough life, before my dad put his foot down. He did not send mom to come back to get me. He came himself shaking his head. "Gather your things you are leaving." On the way to the car he lectured me about how mom and me had better to pull it together. Because we were killing him faster than the coal dust ever could. Mom, greeted me with open arms. I would have told her how I learned to plant flowers while I was at Sabras. Sabra also lacked the maternal instinct. She possessed more of a survival of the fittest instinct than a whole den of lions. She wanted to plant hydrangea bushes all over her yard. She chose me to help her. I was too lazy to beat a shovel into the ground. I did it anyway. Just because her other two children were preoccupied with their rebellious teenage spirit. She gave me specific instructions on how deep to dig. I was not an experienced gardener but I knew I was digging way too deep to plant some bulbs. I shoveled with all of my might going deeper and deeper with each shove. The dirt flying gave me some sort of peace of mind. I was conquering the earth. The dirt spit the earth up the further I pushed the shovel. I was taking all of my frustrations out the further and faster I dug.

I hoped what I discovered was some kind of Civil War artifacts. At first glance, I thought it was remains of a family pet. I was neither an horticulture or forensic expert, the more dirt I uncovered. I screamed so loud I frightened my own self. During the joy of shoveling I dug too deep. Sabra shot out the door like a missile. She snatched the shovel from my hand thinking I had seen a snake. She looked down in the hole exposing her secret. "Go inside get you something to drink and sit down." She almost toppled me over running in the house behind me heading for the trash bags.

Through the window I watched as she dug the roots off of the bones and bagged the secret up. She carried the trash bag to the dumpster in the alley. I was speechless and numb. I was in shock she handled it so calmly. I was frozen to my seat. Scared to move. Scared to speak to the woman who held the shovel so tightly. Sabra came into the living room clutching an ice cold 7-up. The frost from the can had the letters blurred. She took a guzzle and sprawled out exhaustingly in the recliner. "Muffy, forget what you saw." She said it more like a threat not a sentence. Years ago I got pregnant by a walk away Joe. I already had two kids here that I could not support and you down the road, I did not have an opportunity to support. My mother would have killed me if I would have showed back up at her doorstep with a big belly she would have murdered me. So I opted for drinking gin and castor oil." By this point I am at the edge of my seat trying to solve the mystery of whose bones I had just uncovered. "Muffy, castor oil did not help me. I had no choice I had to beg God please get this baby out of me. Nothing happened. Two months later at roughly 26 weeks pregnant I went into labor. I gave birth to that dead baby upstairs in the bathroom. I took her out and buried her in the yard because nobody knew and the funeral home would have charged me for a proper burial and I just do not have that kind of money."

"THAT'S MY SISTER!" I screamed. Sabra replied if you don't be quiet you are going to be laying beside her. "Do you understand?" She never gave me the opportunity to to answer yes or no we just mutually agreed without uttering a word that I did indeed understood. I listened in silenced while my mind danced back moments earlier. Stillborn huh? I thought. I found it peculiar that the skull was twisted from the spine. Sabra, could have set there for weeks and extended that hug I longed for but I was smart enough to know if my baby sister had of been born dead there would have been no need to snap her neck. The reason I could not tell Mom about my gardening was only because Sabra, threatened my life, but because no emotions were ever allowed to be expressed in our household. Secrets were never to be told not ever if they were buried in the front yard. Especially if they were buried in the front yard.

There were so many things I wanted to tell mom. I just kept it inside like a time capsule. I was so delighted when I met Sabras mom. She had been the one who gave me the majority of care when I was little. I had no memory of her. There she sat at the head of her kitchen table. A plump woman wearing the trophy of being such a good cook around her waist. She was chain smoking Pall Malls. Her long bright red nails curved. Her Snow White hair looking as if it were cotton instead of hair. Her crispy wrinkles were enhanced because of her dark complexion. Those big beautiful blues looked like topaz in the center of her face. She was the sponsor of these eyes most of us have. I wondered would that be my face in fifty years? Minus the cigarettes. Stevie, was not the cookie baking grandmother other people had. Stevie's , words were mostly vicious as she spit out truths. She bordered wicked and bitter. Yet, she still entertained people with her wit and charm or belting out a beautiful song. She had a Kitty Wells in her pipes. She was the matriarch of this family. If you needed something she is where you went. Her sisters and nieces and nephews were had all been recipients of her saving grace. And they had also been the victim of her cruelty.

When I was two years old, Sabra was on a weekend date with Scooter and Allisons dad. The weekend date lasted all week. Back then people left their front doors unlocked, especially in small rural

towns. Stevie was in the kitchen cooking, while I played in the living

room floor. The screen door flies open and Mom, storms inside

snatching me up in her arms. I could just see my tiny petite mother

scurrying with my heavy metal legs struggling as she ran to the car

where her oldest son Nick, was waiting with the engine running.

Mom, was prepared with a pistol. Stevie, not only had a reputation

of being a great cook and vicious tongue. She also had the

reputation of being violent. If she would have come through and

saw what Mom was doing no doubt she would have ripped my tiny

mom to shreds. Stevie came through to find an empty living room.

She searched the street hoping that I had just escaped out of the

front door. Her gut instinct knew exactly who had taken me. She

called the police to no avail.

Due to the fact that, dad was in the same club with the county

sheriff, Stevies pleas for my return went unheard. Myra and her

other sister, Adele was not even allowed to see me.They would walk past my new house in hopes to see me in the yard. Mom, cut

all ties with that side of my family. The uncles, aunts and cousins I

knew and loved were soon erased from my memory bank. There

were dozens of them too. Stevie was the eldest child of a family of

nineteen. Great aunts and cousins were in and out of her house all

of the time. Never a dull moment. Stevie also shared Sabras opinion

of Mom. They detested her. Stevie blurted out cruel comments.

Although she was not above slinging a racial slur out. She found it to

be the upmost of white trashery that my dad had rumored to be

affiliated with the Klan. In small towns, gossip is the gospel so it is

never any need to plead a defense.

Mom, honestly believed what she had done to get me was right.

They loved me. They adored me. Each and everyone of them. I was

always different from them. I loved to read. That is an entire family

who honestly cared more about what the neighbors thought than

what the people in their own household felt. Sabras family was the

total opposite. They were flowing with emotion. Most of it

negative, but you never had to wonder what somebody was feeling, that is for certain. When Mom, got upset with my dad she would send him to the grocery store for items she knew he was struggle to find. She would wipe down cabinets to express her aggravation. Sabra, beat her ex husband with an iron skillet. Stevie stabbed Allison and Scooters dad. That family never has to question anything.

Since Sean, is now property of the state, my apartment is filthy once more. It is always the same issues with me. I am wrinkled. I wear nice name brand wrinkled clothes and I am fine with that. He was a clean freak. He cleaned up after me. He said "He was not about to live in filth no matter how trashy he lived his life." Now he is gone and my laundry has a musky scent to it. Jewel and Myra both team up on me explaining to me the washing machine does the work. But they do not seem to realize I have to lug and tug heavy laundry baskets to a laundry mat. Most of the time I read while I am there or I get bored and remove the clothes from the dryer while they are still damp. I don't fold them or put them away

so it is difficult for me to determine what is clean and what is dirty.

Myra, said I need beat for that. She may be right.

I still go to the meetings because it is a condition of my parole.

When I got put out of the shelter I did not violate enough to go back

to prison, instead my parole officer refused to put in for my

discharge papers until further notice. I like the fellowship with the

others that struggle the way that I do. Where we differ is: they have

a will and a want to stop. I have plans to be high as I receive my

discharge papers. Our remote area of the world does not deter the

demons in these mountains. A few years ago the city wanted to

shoot for an aesthetic appeal. They raised property taxes and did

fundraisers to brick our sidewalks and hang bountiful blooming

hanging baskets from the lamp post. It does appeal to the eye. But

if you look down you will see homeless people who wrap

themselves tightly in brown wool blankets they have stolen from

the homeless shelter. They use their backpacks for pillows. Parking

lots and alleys all serve as campgrounds for them.

In the daylight hours those red brick streets are the gateways for attorneys to get from their offices to the court houses to cop pleas for the innocent and not so innocent. Funny thing about an Appalachian judicial system; everybody is guilty. The city council turns a blind eye to these big city problems in a small town. They really believe a fresh coat of paint on an old building and a hip pub on the corner will disguise what it is really like here. The pill epidemic is equivalent to the locust plague. I do not feel sorry for those that struggle with their addiction. They have a daily choice to make like I do. For now, I am choosing not using. Until I get off of paper. Jewel, disagrees with me. She was a entrepreneur in the cocaine industry. After her release she got involve with feeding the homeless. She says "Muffy, if I were to die tomorrow, I want to be remembered as making some kind of difference in this world, no matter how small."

Her opinion is these addicts are different from the ones that roam big city streets. Here they have no reason to get clean. Nothing to fight for so they get caught in a trap.

CHAPTER EIGHT

This morning my worst nightmare became a reality. At exactly 11:34am my phone rang. It was Wava. She had not spoke to me in years. Her voice was crackled with tears in her throat. She was blunt and to the point. "Mom, is gone." I heard her words but they still did not register in my mind. I thought if I could ask her questions her words would change. Maybe.. just maybe I thought I had misunderstood. It was a logical to think she meant mom was out of state visiting her sister. Each question I spewed out got the same answer. "She is gone." Her tears weld up to the stop and she whispered "Mom is home with daddy and Jesus." I screamed and cussed. I filled with ire. Vicious rage took over me. I was not ready

to be orphaned. I was not ready to never pick up the phone and

hear her sweet voice. And go to sleep knowing that the only person

in this world who loves me unconditionally is praying for me. I

understand as a Christian mom reached the highest possible goal.

Resting in the arms of Jesus. None of that was helping at that

moment. It does not make the emptiness in my spirit go away. I feel

like the foot of a giant is pressing on my chest. My mommy is gone,

it may sound selfish but I want her here.

Uneasy thoughts about what is going on in my moms living room

right now. I watch it from my mind like its is playing on a movie

screen. My brothers and sisters that I grew up with and their

children are crying going through photo albums. Wava and Polly

probably came in toting pans of food. While I was smashing in the

walls and busting mirrors, they were in their kitchens frying and

baking. My brothers are on the porch rocking their hurt away in

mom and dads wooden rockers. One of them is hoping that I will be bold enough to show up. Mom is not alive any more to protect me from their opinions of me. Collectively, they all agree I am no good because of how I did not raise my own children and burdened them with my responsibilities. I want to go there. My mind is this dark pit and I know better than to go. Just like they feel some type of way about me I feel some type of way about them. I am grateful for them. They took excellent care of me when I was a child. They take excellent care of my children. That does not mean I am fond of their bland personalities. Laughter, amongst them is a rarity. I do not have the sibling bond with them like they have amongst themselves. Polly was in the eighth grade when I came along. I am different, I do not fit in. They never make a secret. They hide my existence from my children. Champ is being raised to believe that I am a distant psychotic cousin. I am not the only absentee there. My biological father would not dare to show up there. He hadn't spoke a word to mom since the day she kidnapped me.

Deep down inside I would like to see him at moms funeral. I would like ask him why did he hate me so much that he turned on his own mother for loving me? I have questions that Sabra has already answered for me. But... I want..need to hear it from him. Sabra, is a straight shooter and she does not sugarcoat anything. Her honesty may be brutal, but at least she is honest. Sometimes I believe she only tells the truth so she can inflict hurt on others. Every minute with this foot on my chest feels like hours. I am scared to go to sleep because I am afraid to wake up and not know what to do. I have never breathed a breath in this world without her support. I do not know how to live without her. I have never felt anything close to this kind of pain.

A week has passed since Wava called. It feels like it was only minutes ago. One benefit of having multiple personality disorder is I have numerous voices in my mind. They have been occupying my time so I have evaded feeling this nightmare. It as if I am breathing with only one fluid filled lung. I slap the side of my head to make the voices stop after they have rustled up my brain too much. Polly, acted as if she were giving me some kind of honor by extending an invitation to the service to me. It was a surprise that they notified me of the arrangements and added my name to the obituary. They knew mom, adored me from the day I entered into this world. First grandchild. Mom, loved all of her children. She just loved me a little bit more. I needed more. Polly, acts like she can continue living her perfect life as long as she continues to cover up her family secrets. Wava, stepping up for my son, she fell in love with him the second he was born. She wanted him as her own, anyway. The way I see it is I did her the favor. I am by no means a psychological expert but from what I have seen I do believe it is strange to want someone else's baby as your own. My older brother, Todd is in his mid fifties. He has no life experience after he graduated salutatorian of his class he took a job at a local grocery store. No children, no wives ex or otherwise. Just him with his judgmental belief system.

The best relative I have on both sides is my quadriplegic

brother,Will, Maybe, he figures there is no need to fight with me

because he has accepted I will never change. He knows I struggle

with demons beyond my control. The things that happen in my

mind surpasses what most people can imagine. Or maybe he never

loses up that the same little chubby legged cherub face girl mom

snatched up from the meanest woman in three counties will

somehow overcome and be intelligent and lovable once more. He

does not condone or tolerate my foolishness neither does he judge

it. My brother has overcome so many obstacles I suppose it is hard

for him to imagine not everyone can conquer the obstacles the the

way he does. He learned to drive a car using his mouth. He has

never missed a day of work. He is a better parent to Ella mae sitting

down than I ever was standing up.

Sabra, and Myra hated my mom. Those feelings were not subsided

she died either. They refused to attend her funeral, I understand

that. I expect no less of them. They didn't like her alive so they show no concern for her death. Although each of them in their own way extended their condolences to me. Sabra, by telling me. "Ol gal you are going to have to pull it together now because nobody alive is going to do for you what she did." Myra called and asked me if there is anything she can cook for me. I told her I believed cabbage rolls would help. Once more, Myra took her last few dollars and went to the grocery store and prepared a feast. Instead of going to eat that delicious meal. I went off with Piper and lost my appetite. Myra cussed me until she ran out of breath. Accused me of being disrespectful. Finally, it was either showtime or showdown. And the last time I would see my mom on the earth had approached. No more evading. No more high to numb my face and my heart.

Jewel drove me. There she was dressed to the nines. She is always dressed to the tilt. Even if it is just going to Walmart. When funeral happens there she is outshining the pastors wife. Her hair pulled up into a French twist. Her curls spraying upwards like a still firework. She puffs on a stinking Newport while she searches for a place to park. That is when it dawns on her that she hates funerals. Before she speaks it, I see the sentence on her face. "I can not go in there." She seen the hearse and panicked which made us both laugh. "Muffy, go inside and pay your respects and I am going to sit out here and wait, I will wait all day if I have to." She pulls up to the bottom of the steps to the church. Without another thought. It was do or die. I jump out of the car and climb the steps like a hungry ape. I lack gracefulness. My anxiety is making me sweat in this powder blue wrinkled dress. The wrinkles still do not hide the pink sprays of flowers throughout the dress. Sabra, picked me the ugliest thing she possibly could find. I know she probably did it on purpose. I enter the double doors and the ushers guide me to the opposite rows of pews from where my entire family is sitting. They look like they have just stepped out of a sitcom from the fifties. Drab, black, gray and navy blue blends the dismal scene to my right. I sit in the back and watch the humans that I gave birth too. Their actions and reactions and look for similarities. I hope and silently pray none of my characteristics imposed themselves on those children.

Nobody has noticed me back here, I feel like my presence is a nuisance to them. Suddenly, Pollys eyes move from her tissues to me. Here she comes for me. Her prim and proper priss that she can not help makes her way back to me. "Muffy, why are you not up here with us?" I explain the usher told me where to sit and I did not want to go against his direction. Her already saddened face turns to pity. She reaches to hug me and takes my hand and leads me in the center of my brothers and sisters. I feel like a bull in a china shop walking behind her. Everyone's eyes are on me. I am so terribly nervous. My children look at me like I am a distant cousin from out of town. Mom, told me once that my name is not allowed to be mentioned in the homes of my children. Forbidden. I notice that all three may have a different address and call a different woman mom. They all share my crystal blue eyes. Thanks Stevie. The pastor has a solemn look on his face. Mom, is laying at peace front and center. The lights shine on her face. She has a smile on her face as if she has found peace and tranquillity. I have not seen her smile in

years.

It takes every ounce of composure that I have to not jump in the

casket with her. I want to die too. My knees are weak and I can not

control my sobs. I pay no attention that my wails are the loudest in

the church. Everyone in here, has someone to lean on except for

me. Mom, was all that I had to lean on. My unconsoled shoulders

jerk as I fight to quiet down. The voices in my head are vibrating like

a train giving warning a crash is coming. I jump to my feet and run

towards the double wood doors. Nobody follows behind me. I see

Jewell whizzing out of the parking space and pulling up by the steps

for me. She whizzed out like I was leaving a bank robbery, not a

Methodist funeral.

"Muffy, it is okay we are about to go to Dairy Queen, you love the

Dairy Queen." I feel as second of relief then sob "I ran out of moms

funeral." She always knows what to say to help she gets that from

her mother Myra. "Muffy, funerals are not for the dead. The dead are in heaven, funerals are for the family of the dead. And... you do not even like them." At the red light she looks at me and says "come to think about it, you do not even like that church." I feel better and my crying has ceased but I still feel like a wimp. I should have handled it better. Eating the peanut butter parfait is the only relief I have had all week. The comfort food freezes the back of my throat. I bust out into laughter. Jewels arched eyebrows raise and her green eyes seer at me. "Polly.." I am laughing so hard I can not finish my sentence. I think another serious thought. Then find my words. "Polly, thinks she is getting a chunk of an inheritance." Jewell squints her emerald green eyes back at me and replies. "See, this is why none of them like you." We laugh in unity when I say "I do not really care." On the way home the emptiness in my heart swells up. It hits me I no longer have a home base to return to. All of my good childhood memories are being lowered into the ground this minute. Every one has someone to go home to, except for me. I dread the loneliness before I get there. No matter how despicable Jewels husband is at least he will be at home when she gets there.

Sean, was the best man I have ever had. I miss him something terrible. Yes, he stayed high more than he stayed sober. Yes, he was a manipulative addict and succeeded well at fitting the addict stereotype. He was all of those descriptions and more. Yet, he was also, charming and good looking. He showed concern for me. Even high he catered to me the best he could. He never once raised a hand to me. I think that is only because he was not free long enough. Perhaps he would have tried to break my bones, my spirit and my teeth like so many others had in the past if he was not always in and out of jail. My brother Scooter, is also a frequent flyer as well. One time we did the math and counted that Sean had actually shared a pod with him more days than he shared an apartment with me. I can not understand why they use jail as a place to rest. I hated every day of that place. I am not cold natured but I never felt warm in there the entire time. It's drab, and excessively loud. The rules change daily without letting anyone else know. How do you expect exemplary inmates when they do not get the memo yesterdays rules are not what we follow today. The thin

mats that they refer to as mattresses are not at all comfy, and

especially if you are a healthy woman such as myself. I am not a

housekeeper or a cook but I can cook better than the food they

serve. You absolutely have to be told what it is because looking at it

does not help determine. The putrid smells would gag a maggot. I

watched a tiny girl twenty years old succumb to an ear infection in

there. The health care sucks. An ear infection should be easily

treated. You lose any dignity you had left. There is no privacy. It is

everything horrible in one place. Yet, they continue to go in and out

like it is the Hilton.

CHAPTER NINE

Sitting alone like this makes me feel like I have survived the

apocalypse. I have a lot of spare time on my hands. My hours at the call center have declined. I am still in the lead of sales though. I love the fact I can work and I have somewhere important to me to be at everyday. Mom, was very proud when I told her I finally got a job. She was even more proud when we realized I was able to thrive on those phones. Months and months have passed since mom went to heaven. I say it like that so that I do not have to mention my mom and death in the same sentence. It still feels like yesterday. Time does not heal all wounds. Last night, I weathered the cold and walked to the Fellowship hall for a meeting. Sterling was there. Phyllis was not. Since I had nothing to lose I thought I would step out of my shell. I approached him, as if I was in need of a sponsor. I tried to keep my cool and act as if I was not aware of Phyllis not being present. Adding to my many lengthy list of flaws, I lack couth. "Where is that hideously ugly woman you always have by your side." I could not believe I said it out loud. Oh well it was too late to take it back. His deep raspy voice responded, "Oh, so you do not like Phyliss?" He shrugged his shoulders and said "neither do I, anymore." My whole spirit instantly became delighted. Now, I have hope. Another much in need addict interrupted our conversation. He excused himself and wandered away. Slipping through my fingers once more.

My mind drifts from memories of Sterling making eye contact with me and dreams of our future together. I see us at the ocean jumping the loud roaring waves as they crash against our ankles. Taking those evening strolls through the sand like I see couples on television do. I currently lack confidence, to delve into pursuing him in all of my waking hours. Although I want to. I have to realize what do I have that would make him want me? Beautiful crystal blue eyes, and a flawless complexion thanks to my Indian ancestry, and intelligence? Yes, I am equipped with that. I also bring with me the baggage of my past. I am sure he will not mind that one bit because he has one too. I also come with voices in my head that do not match any familiar faces. I also have a unkept hair style, broad shoulders with bad posture that supports my almost deformity large breast. DNA rolling through my veins that makes me like to fight a lot. Yeah, come to think about it why would he not want a woman like me. I will fight men too so I would not mind to defend him if I ever had too.

The phone rings breaking my concentration. Alisha and me talk for hours. Small town gossip is always the best. Everyone is famous in a small town. We know everyone's business and their birthdays and what they got as gifts. It's kind of a Mayberry with a twist of a rough New York borough. People see these wondrous mountains that reach the skies. Always picturesque scenery going through winding roads looking up to see trees as old as forever blocking the rays of the sun. Underneath the shades from the tree limbs is also some shady behavior. Alisha prides herself as an authority of knowing everyone's business. I am sure it is not all fact. She makes it sound as if it is. Gossiping is therapeutic for us. Concentrating on other peoples business distracts us from our lonely bland lives. Alisha is not attractive yet she boast about how good she looks. She is 4'11" and desperate to feel tall. She looks for love in the arms of men who are already married. That has to be hurtful that she is always number two. She never lets on. The devious nature in her relationships makes her feel special. I do not judge her for that because I would not let a marriage stop me from a date either. Alisha, does not drink nor has she ever done any drugs whatsoever. She has no empathy for addicts.

I wish that me and Allison, could chat for hours on the phone like me and Alisha do. Allison, is always on the go. She does not let no grass grow under her feet. She maintains a job no matter if she never has anything to show for it. Getting her to go somewhere with me is like pulling teeth. She claims my driving terrifies her. When my dad, bribed me to leave Sabra's with a car. I kept the roads hot. Allison was my copilot. If she was not in school she was in the passenger seat of my red Chevette. One night, I picked up another friend first and then went to pick up Allison. Allison is never ready on time. Her clock ticks slower than everyone else's and mine ticks faster. I am always early. Allison dashed into the back seat and we sped off into the night. That Chevette was full of laughter and loud music. Allison and me have a unique relationship where we bicker over everything. She feels is always right and there is never no explaining any other way. Our laughter turns into another quarrel between us. I felt like she should give me two dollars for gas. She felt like she should keep her two dollars.

I was distracted by the argument and I pulled out from the intersection. My little red Chevette was no match for the semi tractor trailer that barreled through us. When the news aired the coverage of the wreck my car looked as if King Kong had stepped through it. I did not hear the screams. I heard the screeching sound of metal colliding. I was knocked out instantly. I did not feel or hear the second impact when the truck jack knifed. I had a concussion and two broken ribs. My passenger Christina, she still suffers limited mobility and uses a walker to aid her with her steps. Her pelvis was shattered into hundreds of pieces. Allison was ejected from the backseat. They found her lifeless body 1176 feet away from the wreckage. The firefighters who arrived on the scene first placed a sheet over her body to keep traffic from gawking at her young lifeless body. The ambulance service sent for a body bag as they were lifting Allison to slide her in the bag. She started breathing. No CPR, no anything just like some sort of miracle she started to breathe.

She has always been a rough neck. When she rose up and saw that body bag for her, she went into a dramatic panic. They had to sedate her to calm her down. The doctors explained to Sabra that they would have to shave Allisons beautiful blonde hair to remove the glass from her head. Sabra could not imagine her beautiful daughter being tormented with half of her bald head. So she refused. They worried that people would tease Allison. She wears the memory of that night on her left cheek. A deep scar that looks like she has been sliced with a box cutter. Sabra was so furious at me until the insurance check came. Jewel has theorized that night. She believes a scar is not the only remnant from the wreck Allison bares. She says traumatic brain injury is probably the reason you can not reason with Allison. Christina and I lost touch after that night. She remembered everything vividly. Her family tried to have me charged with attempted murder. I was distracted. I did not mean to hurt anyone. Christina made a statement once she came out of the coma, that my last words before I pulled onto the highway was "Bitch I will kill you."

I was just rambling words. I did not mean to kill nobody. I was very and still am bitter that Christina attempted to sabotage me. Allison will ride with me but only if I am the last resort.

Allison, not only carries a grudge from the wreck. During the three years I actually had custody of Rhiannon. Allison was at my nasty apartment a lot. Isn't that how it is supposed to be little sister hanging out a big sisters apartment? I lived 8 duplex doors down from Sabra and Allison. She would stop by on her way to school and scramble eggs for Rhi. Most of the time she would bring the eggs with her. If dad did not grocery shop for me, I would have naked refrigerator. Allison loved Rhi and Rhi loved her. Allison was the biggest fun for her. So sweet and kind. When Rhi was around we saw a different Allison. The scraper the vain worried about what the town was going to say about her was gone. We had a fun loving personal clown. She would brush Rhis hair. When she would cuss me for not combing and caring for Rhis hair it would infuriate me and I would take it out on Rhi. I jerked her tangles through the comb. If she cried I would tap the brush on her head. She would cry even harder. One evening I was teasing and spraying my hair when Rhi, would not quit screaming. Maybe she was hungry, maybe she wanted attention. Maybe she wanted something. Nothing Allison could do would soothe her. She came out of her room squalling. By that point I had enough of the noise. I slung the Aqua Net hairspray can aim for her stomach but I missed and it hit her in the temple. She tumbled down thirteen steps, screaming even louder. I screamed for her to shut up. She still would not. Allison, became enraged. She did not know what to do. She knew at that time she could not take me. She called Polly. And told her what she had seen

me do, that was the last day I was a mother to Rhi.

I loved Rhi all darlingly dressed up. I was proud of her beauty. An

image of an all American girl. I just lost patience with getting a wild

three year old tamed long enough to keep her blonde tresses shiny

and tangle free. I did not have the desire to keep her clothes clean.

Allison would bag Rhis child stained clothes and tote them up the

street to Sabras. Mom, always thought I was washing her clothes

and I never told her any different. Allison would stop by each

morning on her way to school to cook Rhi breakfast. Allison was

always older than her age. Her maturity and long legs made it easy

for her to pass as a nineteen or twenty year old but in reality she

was only fourteen years young. I suppose her child like years

languished, because she constantly providing care for Scooter.

Sabra, was no mother not to me and not to them. She gave them all

she had she just never had much. She struggled financially and

mentally. As I watch Sabra now with Jewels kids and I hardly can stand it. Jewel and her daughters deserve the best of everything. I wish Sabra had loved us and my children like that.

I feel resentment swelling up whenever Sabra, raves about those precious little girls. I understand that is her duty as a great aunt. I just do not know why she, has to be the, greatest aunt. Sabra, talked to me and Allison about how easy it is to love them. The point that she made was it was none of our business and that we were horrible and those little girls are precious. Jewel tells it a different way. She said. "Sabra, is not responsible for my kids daily. She does not have to hustle to keep their power on, and a roof over their head. Now, she has an opportunity to love kids in a way she could never afford to love her own." That makes sense to my brain but my heart still aches that she was not like that with us or Rhi. Maybe if we would have been born kind and caring and pretty like Jewel our mother would have loved us the way she loves her and hers. We are the oddities. Allison is blonde with bright ivory blemish free skin. She is tall. Those features alone should make her outshine anyone. Her upshapely body and fierce attitude hides any beauty.

She is quick to start fights and even quicker to finish them. She can

not beat me. She has tried.

CHAPTER TEN

Last night, I went to a meeting at the Fellowship home. Meetings

there tend to bring me comfort. It brings me peace to know

compared to the people housed there, I live in the land of milk and

honey. Some of those people have never held a job. They have

never owned a car. Some have never even drove a car. My chaotic

spirit is tried a true to the saying a rolling stone gathers no moss. I

have always wanted to keep the roads hot. Some of those people

that attend those meetings have just stagnated like mosquitoes

hovering over a swamp. I have roamed to the Midwest and the

south. I always end up back here in this same rut, but at least I have traveled the interstate before. I have that in common with Sterling.

He is cultured. He finally noticed me last night. He shot me a wink at

first I thought he had dust in his eyes. No, it was a real wink. I shot

out of that building, fumbling for my keys as if I had hit BINGO. I do

not pick up quickly to social cues. I am way too paranoid for that. If

someone is too kind to me, I think they are patronizing me. If they

treat me like everyone else, I do not feel special. If they treat me

like everyone else, I feel unnoticed. If people treat me distant

because they do not know me, it makes me feel unwanted. No

matter how my mind deciphers people and their reactions, I know

last night I finally broke the ice. I called Jewel as soon as I flopped

on my couch. I wasted no time pushing the couch cushion back in

its proper place.

That wink showed me I stand a chance with him and that is all I

have wanted. I know once he gives me a chance we will vibe on an

intellectual level. To get a better understanding of him I snooped

through his mailbox once. His last name holds a status of

prominence. Jewel accuses me of stalking him. I do not think researching a persons interest is stalking. She does not understand those of us who have been shopping in the women's section since the sixth grade can not just bat an eyelash and it be adored by men. She probably has never had to go the extra mile to feel loved. His wink made me flushed all over. The hair on the back of my neck stood up. How will I hide my crazy? If he gives me more than a wink. Stevie always used to say our kind of crazy is the worst. "The best crazy is to be so far gone, you can not realize you are crazy. But.. to know you are different, that is by far the worst." Stevie, may not have been a cookie baking apron wearing grandmother. But her rough raw savage nature, has helped me. I was terrified of her. To see how she pierced her clawed finger nails into the arms of her loved ones, petrified me. I knew if it took all the strength in me I would never lose control of my emotions around her. My crazy was not nearly as wicked as hers. She cussed her sons equally as she equally cussed her daughters. Nobody did anything right according to her.

I miss my mom something terrible. I cringe when I see mothers and daughters out together. Envious is an understatement. I want my mom back living on this earth. She may not have been fun to hang out with like Sabra, or a best friend. She was my mother, not my friend. She was my rock the foundation for my life. I would like to say I picked up on some of her conservative values. I did not. I never sided with the judgmental views or the way the church members gossiped about other members and their failures. But there was so much more to them than dress clothes and gossip. They were prayer warriors, they believed in something and tried to guide their children in a good path, to keep us from living a life of unsavory consequences as I do. She went far and beyond to pacify my needs and my wants. It hurts so much that she is no longer here for me to lean on. I never felt different around my mom. I felt, loved, normal and fortunate. I wish I could go back and spend every second of my life that I jumped out of my bedroom window to run off with boys with her. I wish that I could hear her pray for my well being once more. The horrible thing about grief is you never get over it you just learn to carry a heavy heart and live with it.

I got my discharge papers, from the parole board. I have money left over from every paycheck. Yet, my delusional mind is still holding me a prisoner. Falling asleep is agony for me. Every bad thought crosses my mind when I shut my eyes. If it is too quiet in this apartment I hear voices. I try to turn the tv on to tune them out as I read True Blood trilogies. None, of that seems to be helping. I never miss work no matter how much sleep I miss. From time to time I escape my demons with a small bag of cocaine. No matter if I spend one hundred dollars or six hundred dollars on the high, it never seems to be enough. Despite sleep deprivation, drug addiction and a touch of schizophrenia, I am still the reigning queen of the telemarketers. I have work friends. Even though mom is gone on to her resting place I have family and Alisha and Piper yet I am still lonesome. I do not understand why I had to be born like this or develop this. I get mad at God for making me destined for failure. I hid my sadness and pathetic behavior by trying to make jokes and laugh with everyone. Even when the engine blew up in my car, I cussed but then laughed. I had no idea where to put oil or that you had to change oil in cars.

Once again, there I was stranded with an open hood while cars whizzed past me in the rain. Nobody to call, nobody to stop. Soft spring drizzle tapped on my shoulders as I walked four miles to Myras house. After the third mile I could feel the muscles stretching in my legs. Myra, cussed me for not calling her to come and pick me up. My cell phone was dead. Then she cussed me for being too sorry to charge my phone. Her house smelled so good as the smell of chili and homemade cornbread permeated through. Her couch is always so inviting. Which is why I invited myself not to leave. Sabra and Myra now take turns taking me and picking me up from work. I spend my paychecks like a teenager, food, candy and clothes. I am troubled sitting still. Waiting for life to happen slobbed on the couch. The food and snacks only appeases me for brief moments. I had to find a man. Any man. I found a nice man, he is his mothers caregiver and works at Lowes part time. Lewis, he is nice to cuddle next to while watching sitcoms at his mothers house. My attention span does not make it worth my while to watch movies. That is why love to read. I love it when the words come to life in my brain. He is a member of the church and would not dream of touching me the way that I need him to. His faith is important to him. So I watch my mouth, and do not say much in fear that I may let G.D fly out of my mouth. He is a gentleman. Too gentle.

Funny how life happens so abruptly. In my life I have learned to adapt. I went from driving myself to work and wherever I wanted to go, to bumming rides to and from work. Now, no work. I was laid off. The company lost their contract from the company I was working on. Now I can collect unemployment and be bored all day again. This hurt me through my soul. There was no notice, no warning no workplace full of gossiping fear that this was going to happen. Just a note on the door and a key card that declined entry.

I sobbed and cried as Sabra sat in wonderment as to why I had not

went in the building. I screamed, cussed, kicked the door and

pounded on the shatterproof glass door. Sabra pulled up to where I

was standing throwing a full rant of rage hissy fit. "Get in the damn

car you idiot" she added some more explicit words to that

sentence. I cowered down and did as she instructed. "Stop all of

that snotting, that's gross." I turned my anger toward her because

she was being so callous. I can not remember what I uttered back.

Whatever I said our morning was not a peaceful drive through the

fog after that. She grabbed my arm and twisted it. I wanted to sock

her back in the face. But I did not. In one sense it appeased me that

she cared enough about me to correct me. "Muffy, you can not

whoop me. You can not beat me. I will pull this car over and tie you

to the trunk. You ain't a Betty bad ass, like you claim, you are a big

cry baby whining face."

She pulled into to a Tudors Biscuit World as if we were a mother and daughter eating after a morning of shopping for shoes. Sabra's whole family is like that as if violence is normalcy. Perhaps to them it is. To us it is. My mother would have got out of the car tried the door, called inside and tried to resolve the issue but not Sabra. She cussed at him and then asked "what are you getting?" I really had no appetite but I ate anyway. I dabbed my biscuits into my gravy and silently cried on the inside. I knew if I started expressing any emotion Sabra would at best leave me sitting at the table or at worse reach across the table and smash me like a roach running from light. No car, no Sean, no job and nobody to love me. I felt so alone. I contemplated suicide for the first time in my troubled life. Sure, I had thought about it previous times but never like that. My suicidal thoughts slowly became a suicidal fantasy. I entered into my empty, dismal and dirty apartment. The sour smell of the sheets hugged me as I slept and slept. Before I knew it, the thoughts of killing myself became the only reason I had to wake up each day. I had nothing else to live for except getting the courage to do it.

The morning came that I was bored and nobody I knew was answering the phone for me. Both best friends had busied their lives with their children and jobs and doing all of the things I did not have. I went through the Rolodex in my brain and over and over I got voicemails. Finally, I got my courage. I was thrilled that I had figured out how to escape my chaotic brain. I felt a rush as if I had been sniffing cocaine. I no longer felt weighted by my troubles. I cried because of all of the people that I loved that I knew I would never lay eyes on again. I missed them before I was gone. I called Sabra and she actually answered. The sound of her voice made me sob. I knew it would be the last time I ever heard gentle or harsh words come out of her mouth. I began to miss life and everyone in it. Tears spewed from my eyes like water pipes exploding in frigid temperatures. I was sobbing so hard I could barely breathe. "Muffy, what is wrong with you?" My words were broken and paused as I tried to push my voice through the tears. "I am going to jump off of the bridge and kill myself today." Sabra, had a brief silence. "Are you trying to get attention you silly bitch. What is your problem? Can you not find nobody to terrorize? Do you need help?" Her questions interrogated me for minutes before I could answer. I assumed that when she asked if I needed help, she was meaning a trip to the psychiatric ward at the hospital, a hug or a boost of confidence. Sabra, came through like she always has done. "Why are you calling to tell me? Do you need a ride to the bridge? Muffy, I do not have time for this nonsense. You do not even have a car. How are you getting to the bridge?"

The worlds longest arch bridge just happens to sit eight hundred sixty seven feet in the air. People from neighboring states often park their cars at the edge and take a walk and then the jump to end their demons. Urban legend speaks that if you throw yourself over into the clouds without a parachute your heart will explode before your body smashes to the ground. I whole heartedly wanted to find out if that was true or not. After talking to Sabra, I realized strong people like her, do not, and can not fathom my mental state.

People like her shake it off whatever it is and the move forward regardless if they are functioning on balance or not. I also determined that people like her do not have compassion for those like me. I have never felt so alone in the world.

Wintry dreary days with the clouds blanketing over the sun, combined with arctic temperatures do not help my state of mind. I keep searching inside of me for the strength that Stevie left within us. I think it missed me. My mind is a complete disarray. I have nothing to live for, other than to stay alive to strive for something to live for. Alisha, finally answered the phone and brought me back from my fantasies. "Muffy, please don't die, I need you. You laugh with me, there is nothing you can not overcome. Look at your life. Look at what all you made it through, and if you were to die, I would miss you something terrible." The sincerity in her voice made me cry. This time tears of joy. She loved me like a sister. Alisha has a few sisters but none does she like as much as me. I love her more than my sisters too. She sounds condescending as she makes jokes to lift my spirit. "You were really going to wake up dead?" She asked. I told her how Sabra did not care and how she offered me a ride to the bridge. "Muffy, Sabra is savage you already know that. Why would you even call her you should have known she was going to be on joke time or savage?" She was right. Funny thing is Alisha was raised right down the alley from Sabra so she knew her better than I ever had.

In these small town communities with one red light. We are close. Our neighbors are more like our cousins. We are all family. They raise their children together, their children raise their children together. It is one convenient store, one post office and one library. It's bigger than everyone just knows everyone. We carry secrets and memories for decades just like a real family does. It makes perfectly good logic that Alisha knows Sabras heart and mind better than I would. I crave more cocaine and I can not afford it. Although I can share my most trifling secrets with Alisha that is one that I can not utter a hint about to her. Alisha hates drugs. She hates those that do them and those that sell them. She host a house party once or twice a year. Each time the party always ends stopping early because either someone brought drugs or some drug addict shows up and crashes the party. She knows my history. I would like to say that my best positive friend in the whole world does not pass judgement on me but that would be false. She holds no punches during my actively using binges. She says that there is no way Piper could be my friend if she gives me drugs. Alisha, has never given up hope that I can be somewhat normal, that the children I gave up so many years ago I will be able to see them one day. So when I get high I am disappointing the hope of positivity she has for me. She does not understand, because she has never used. She feels like if the horrid life she lived with an alcoholic abusive mother did not cause her to get high nobody else has an excuse to use drugs either.

CHAPTER ELEVEN

Just like the seasons my state of mind changes and when spring arrives I have the same problems. I just have more pep in my step. I have unemployment benefits and a wonderful although hateful aunt Myra who has taken me in once more. I love being here. Not only because she cooks breakfast four out of seven days and dinner six days a week. Not only because she sweeps and mops every day and washes my clothes and folds them better than any iron could press out wrinkles. She had suffered from nervous breakdowns and severe depression in her life as well. We share the common bond of our minds being interrupted and our state of mind being misunderstood by our family. She copes with cigarettes and Coca Cola and cussing those of us who surround her and annoy her. I mostly get cussed for being lazy. "Speed up, you walk like dead lice is falling off of you" Me dragging my feet seems to annoy her. And when I told her where I went when I borrowed her car she really flipped but I had to tell someone. I told her how I had been crushing on Sterling for years. How much I truly loved him and respected him. She shot me lowered eyebrow looks. From time to time she would interrupt. "Why haven't we ever met him? Why have you not mentioned him? I proceeded with my tale of my adventure and how I went into Sterlings house. Myra assumed that he had let me in. I mean he somewhat did. The door was not difficult to unlock with a credit card.

I searched through his desk, looking for clues to his life. Hopelessly I searched for what he did as hobbies and what books he enjoys to read. I dived into his chest of drawers and searched his shirts for the size so I will I know what to get him when his birthday comes. I snooped through his bank statements and most recent paystubs as if I were a mortgage broker. Then I sat in his recliner and pretended that he was on the couch and made believe the conversations we would have if he had been home. I could smell the vision of me making him a peanut butter pie. I got up and went through the kitchen cabinets searching for the ingredients so motivated I was ready to prepare the pie and leave it in the refrigerator for he returned home from work. Before I left I plopped down on his bed and smelled his sheets, and knew instantly the smell of cool water cologne.

"Are you stupid? Or are you just acting like it?" Myra shouted. She did not understand my desperation of wanting to know Sterling. Then she falls out into loud contagious laughter. "You are dating a man and he does not even know you are dating?" Her rhetorical questioning gave us laughter until she peed her pants and then we laughed some more about that. It is hard for me to articulate without sounding insane why I needed to go visit Sterling. Myra said "Most of the time when people have you over for a visit, the are aware that you are coming over." We laughed some more. I suppose it does sound pretty absurd. I learned a lot about Sterling and how much he loves history. How much debt he has accrued.

Fixating on Sterling helps give me hope to brighter days. Unbeknownst to Myra, she continues to aid me in stalking. She takes me to all of the meetings that he is speaking at. She believes in me. She thinks since she overcome her years of dismal gloom everyone else can to. I use that to my advantage to attend meetings.

She still cusses me out daily, with cuss words full of flavor, in the same tone as Stevie when she would cuss people. Every time she spews colorful swear words at me she is within good reason. I still do not have any interest in any household chores. Myra, can not understand how I became such a slob when I was raised in such an immaculate house. Even when she suffered from depression she was not as messy as me. She stands with a dish towel over her shoulder as if it is a burping cloth. She is always ready to wipe a mess. I like it here. She always has company coming and going. People stopping in to drink coffee and smoke nasty cigarettes. We do not have hours of boredom and it keeps my mind busy and I stay engaged in conversation. Not only that her couch is the most comfortable thing I have ever planted my butt on. She cares for me as if I were one of her children. Although my lifestyle still mimics a rebellious teenager. She keeps me safe. She does not allow me to bring in men to lay up with. Most importantly, she defends me when Sabra starts pointing out all of the reasons that she should put me out. She knows what it going to take to heal my mind, she pushes me to do better each day. "You always have a home as long as I have a home, but I am not going to live forever, so think about that while you are sitting there like a frog on a rock not doing nothing." I just laugh it off because she is healthy as a horse and strong as an ox. She will out live me.

Jewel, is our family mediator. If we need something from someone we ask Jewel to ask them. Sabra loves her more than all three of her children. I love her more like a sister than a baby cousin. Myra, is proud of her and she goes far and beyond to help make sure she never goes back to prison. Myra, has unhealthy fantasies as well.

She wants to kill Jewels husband. We are crazy but not stupid. We know he has put his hands on her. He is a giant compared to her. She looks like a child standing next to him. Jewel may only stand five feet tall, but her personality is five feet nine inches tall. Physically she is no match for that devil that she has devoted her life to. I look at relationships like that and it scares me. I get reminded of that brief moment in time that I was married. I married a man I had met at the fellowship home. We had a quaint small wedding at the Gazebo in the center of the city. I wore white. Alisha was the only friend or family member that came out to support me. Jewel, was serving her prison sentence at the time. She would have been there if it was not for that. She most likely would have went all out and my wedding would have ended up costing and arm and a leg. Perhaps it would have been similar to Shelbys wedding in Steel Magnolias. Robert moved me hours away to the country side that neighbors Washington D.C. it was so awesome at first. I loved him and I even attempted to keep the house clean all except for the

laundry. I hate laundry no love I have ever known has ever changed
that.

Robert appeared to be everything with potential. He was no
Sterling, but he did take a liking to me which eventually blossomed
into a love with me. Robert, did not have much family. He inherited
the wilderness we called home. A winding dirt road curved us to an
older model trailer in the midst of nowhere. Forty-five minutes
from the city. I struggle to maintain a simple apartment in
civilization. I am no Martha Stewart nor do I claim to be. Robert
expected me to, pick apples and make applesauce. I am too
unbalanced to use a step ladder much less a ladder that rises into
trees. When he seen he did not marry a domestic engineer, he
would get angry and go get drunk. The drunker he would get the
madder he would get. He beat on me. My physical strength was no
match for him. He was bigger and stronger. Often times I would
have to cower down. Take the fetal position and cover to block the
kicks and the punches. One sunny fall day, the glare from the

sunbeams reflected on through the windshield. I was struggling to see. Robert got frustrated. He smacked me in my face.

The sun rays went to pitch black and I can not remember what happened next. There was nobody for miles and miles around, to get protection from. I think about it from time to time trying to figure out what really happened that day. I felt the Ford Bronco accelerate. I heard the engine roaring like an angry bear. I remember hearing his voice screaming in terror. Screams that were so terrifying I get chills to this day when I am haunted by the memories. Like a shot of cheap whiskey I could feel the burn of rage in my throat. Later in the evening I was standing in the middle of the trailer and it occurred to me that he did not make it back with me. I blew it off as if he were just out for another night of drinking and prepared for when he came back to take the frustrations of the hangover and his limited funds on my body. The next morning there was still no sign of Robert. Unusual that he did not return. I grabbed the keys to the bronco and trailed off on a mission. I searched local trailer parks. I yelled into the woods. I shouted his

name until my throat felt sore. No response. Miles and miles of

nothingness surrounded us. Even wild animals were never seen on

the winding dirt roads. Nothing. Days and days eventually passed no

sign of Robert. He did not have steady for friends for me to contact.

No parents, no siblings. They power company came and shut off

the power for nonpayment. As soon as the truck pulled off I was

following the power truck through the dust.

Maybe I did something to him. Maybe I snapped. Maybe I ran him

down as if he were a vicious beast and left his expired body on the

side of the road like road kill. Logic says to me if that were the case I

would have seen his body lying in pre decay as I searched for him.

Maybe I stabbed him and sped off. Maybe I did not do anything to

him. Maybe he just got tired of beating on me and dealing with my

brinks of insanity. All I know is once I left, I did not carry any

thoughts about him with me. I left all the memories good and bad

in the dust. I only hope that if he is still breathing air on this earth, he learned to keep his hands off of women and alcohol is his worst enemy. I hope I did kill him. I just wish I could remember how I did it. I wish that I could have remembered the thrill of his life leaving his body. The rush of hearing his last gasp of life. I wish I knew if she tried to fight back but for that moment I finally was stronger than him. The look of fear on his face when he transitioned. Maybe his look was tranquil. It is possible that he enjoyed dying finally finding peace. Not worrying about another drink or dealing with another consequence related to drinking. I was not even married long enough to have my named changed from Concord to Dalton. Life for me continued, I bounced around to various couches until I could get on my feet.

I still fear for Jewels safety. I am in fear of my own anger if I knew for a fact her husband hit on her. I know she would tell someone. I know as close nit of a family as we are word would spread faster than a California wildfire. I shut my thoughts away and laugh and talk with her. Her wisdom imprints thoughts to my brain. She knows how to do everything. That is why we all turn to her for solutions

and if she can not figure it out she is not too prideful to ask for help.

Fearless. I know she would confide in Sabra. Sabra is also our go to.

She makes sure things happen when there is no way possible for

them to happen. Together these strong women from their humble

beginnings keep me from losing the rest of my mind. I may fall out

with Sabra. She may not speak in loving tones to us. She may not

show her love with hugs like I wish she would. I know she talks trash

to me because she expects more from me. She sees a potential in

me. She sees what I could be instead of what I am. Sabra, is not an

optimist she is a realest. She is the glass is neither half empty nor

half full type of person. She is a, the glass has water in it, now do

with it what you want type of person.

The reminiscing sessions that are held in the center of Myras living

room always leave me thirsting for more knowledge about the

roots that hold my family tree up. Stories about Stevie and her

sisters amuse me the most. My mind is left to ponder, why if my great aunts were math scholars with no high school diploma what would their lives have been like if they would have had the opportunity to attend a college or university. How, is it possible with no formal education one could remember the exact day August 1, 1980 fell on. Her name was Matilda. Tillie was the only name she would answer to. Those that speak of her memory claim that she could do math so well she could figure up within minutes if today is Saturday October 12 2010 then August 1 had to fall on a Friday. How is that even possible that she never had a career or sent a rocket to space?

They speak with such vivid memories that I can see Stevie, in her younger years wearing a hat and strand of pearls with her fresh coat of bright red nail polish out to snatch the hearts of gentleman suitors. They mainly reflect their memories of her golden buttery biscuits that was a fan favorite of anyone who entered her threshold. I can see the black round worn out pan baking up deliciousness. How she stood over an iron skillet whipping white gravy up with nothing more than a natural ability to know what goes in with no recipe. I leave the subject feeling a sense of pride.

Being able to claim such strength is a honor to me. I wonder what

claim to fame they might have had if they had not have had been

entombed by these mountains.

Perhaps, it could have been the same glory I would have had a

chance at a sane mind. Maybe today I would be an English

professor, or even just the plain ole run of the mill librarian. When I

was younger I did not wasted time of planning for my education.

My brain always absorbed the material I was being taught like a

sponge. I just lost interest after having to deal with the cruelty of

the other students. Eating lunch all by myself got old really fast. Just

me and my vegetables. It gets lonely at the bottom.

Sabra and Myra, both agree that I am a prize too. They compliment

me on my skin tone. How I am always tanned even in the winter.

They attempt to give me beauty tips that will accentuate the

attractive physical features that I have naturally. I pay them no

mind. When I shop I chose comfort over looking nice. I tend to like the way my clothes hang on me like they are still on the hanger. I am top heavy and bras cause me great discomfort. I prefer not to wear them. And if I find myself in a must wear situation. It is a safe bet to gamble I will have one that is comfortable on not one for support. Sabra, berates me for the way my hair sticks up and out like a jellyfish gliding through the sea. I decline her offer to take me to the beauty shop for stylish hairstyles. I have better things to do than sit in a chair for three hours until my butt goes numb.

The gloom and doom always makes its way back into our lives. Abusive men is our generational curse. I cringe when I hear stories of the way that Scooter and Allisons dad beat on Sabra. How that gargantuan man through put her through walls. Gambling, drunkard making their life a living hell each weekend. I'm glad he is saved and sanctified now I just wish that he could have lived that way when he was married to Sabra instead of beating on her like she was equivalent to him in stature. To think she still loves him to this day. She had dated everything from vagrants to doctors but none has ever seem to replace the love she has for him. Yet, they call me

insane.

CHAPTER TWELVE

My unstable mood swings and uncontrolled temper has once again

caused me to be kicked out. This time it was the fellowship home. I

loved that place. That is where I could go and be myself and not

worry about being judged because at the end of the day my crimes

and addiction scale less than the majority of those that seek shelter

there. Perhaps my last outburst was fueled by jealousy. Phylis, is to

blame for why I have a lifetime ban. I have watched her and the man of my dreams go on again and off again. This is a time that they are on again. I was getting annoyed by the way she was sitting with her tiny frame and perfect posture. I took my attention off of her and gazed at Sterling. I was zoned out focusing on his messy desk and bookshelves. I felt comforted by the way he left his soft bed unmade, and how he had a couple of piles of dirty clothes in a corner not in a basket. All of that gave me confirmation that we have so much in common it is possible he is my soul mate.

Phylis, continued to sit with her nose in the air. Wrinkle free cardigan hugging her shoulders. The more she sat in perfection the more my jealousy and anger marinated. I strived to keep my cool but my sarcastic come backs interjected every time she spoke. She felt brave enough to speak up on my rudeness. "Muffy, that is enough, everyone in here knows you are only being rude to me because of Sterling." I screamed a list of expletives as I jumped to my feet, darting toward her, planting my open hand across her face. My palm felt like one thousand bees were stinging me. The look of astonishment on her face was worth every second. Sterling, rushed over to intervene so that his precious woman did not take another slap across her face. His bear hug from behind eased my spirit. In reality he was pulling me back from hurting her any further. In my mind, for that split second it was everything I wanted it to be. It was his embrace protecting me from getting into more trouble. They had me sit on the porch while they decided my fate. Phylis, wanted to call the police. She is such a punk. Babs, and Sterling advised her that probably would not be such a good idea. I am very familiar with the practices of that house. I know a lot of dirty deeds that go on in the book keeping methods and other things. The fugitives they harbor. They felt that if I were too be arrested that I may want to even the odds and shut the whole house down. They are right.

Myra, laughed out loud at my craziness. Sabra and Jewel, reamed me. They felt as though I had no right to put my hands on that woman. Sabra, took pity on me after she spoke her opinion. Every night since then we have spent hours on the phone. She is giving me advice on how to get the man I want. She claims men like nice nurturing women. She goes on to tell me that is the problem with the women in our family. "We attract what we are. We are not soft timid women therefore we have to get men who are not nice. That is why we end up living our lives with the men that nobody else would have, the type that their own mothers don't want." Sabra, was definitely beautiful back in her prime. Her physical beauty was enough alone to make any man putty in her hands. Except for the one who she loved the most. I asked her how come he was so good to his second wife who was not nearly as attractive as she was. "Show me a beautiful woman, and I can show you a man who is tired of screwing her." Her bluntness jolted my mind. "He was not always good to her. She is a homemaker. I was not. He partied she waited on him to come home. When he stayed out all weekend on me, he would come home to me on a war path." Sabra, believes that women like us are the problem. She says men like nice, meek women, that tend to be homemakers and put up with all of the extra stuff the mentally ill men we attract dish out.

My intuition tells me that Sterling knows me. He knows my heart

and we are kindred spirits. I am not doing all of this getting to know

him in vain. Thoughts of his name bring joy to my heart. I can see it

in his eyes he is not happy with that stuck up doctor. Plus, she is

ugly. I do these things to help him see that I love him. Sabra, is

trying to help. They do not understand that I have to go the extra.

Men literally fell at Sabras feet. Jewel, could have any man that she

wants. She has always had the pick of the patch. They need to

spend their time judging her for such a rotten pick, instead of

commenting and guiding me to what they believe is normalcy.

Sabra, says "Muffy, you are too smart for any man. Why don't you

go to college or do something productive you are just wasting your

life away." There is no fun in that for me. I love this man. Besides, I

am lonely. I am tired of promiscuous behavior. It is only fun while it

is in presence tense. I crave constant attention. I am certain Sterling

is the one for me. He is all I ever wanted.

Myra, finally got fed up with my lazy antics and put me out. As soon as Jewel, put her Jeep in park we could see the rage on Myras face. She stood at the top of the porch steps with the broom leaning in her right hand. I could smell the bleach and pine sol from the parking lot. As soon as my feet hit the pavement she lifted the broom as if it were a sword and pointed it at me. Her list of expletives ranted on until she was breathless. I did not try to defend myself because I knew I had nowhere else to go. Her rage stemmed from while she was cleaning she found where I had been unsanitary with my feminine products. I kept thinking, oh I will just pick that up later but, I kept forgetting. I left and let her cool down for a few hours. When I returned she was still full of ire. She let me stay another night. We spent all of the next day with her driving me around looking for an apartment and doing to a variety of agencies gathering up the deposit. I had been awarded a HUD certificate in the weeks prior but lacked the gumption to use it. Also, that would mean leaving Myras. She took such good care of me and made my life easy, I procrastinated. Her furiousness left no more time to linger. She placed fear in my heart that she would indeed pierce my heart with the biggest butcher knife she could find. One more night I begged of her. She stood her ground and cussed me some more. I absorbed her words like a sponge. I knew she was right. My messiness keeps me in messes no matter my address. I also knew back talking her could get me kicked to the street. I knew better than to ever ask Sabra if I could stay one night. She made it no secret that I was lucky to get into her heart but never could I stay another night in her house.

She remembered how nasty my apartment would get when my dad used to have to come clean it to keep the bugs away. There was no way she would ever forget that nor allow me to forget that. Plus all me and Allison do is fight if we spend too much time together. I mean physical knock down drag out fights. "Myra, please, if I can stay here one more night, I know I will have a place to live by noon tomorrow." Hesitantly she agreed. The next morning with the funds from the agencies help I was paying my deposit by noon. Sabra, loved when people was moving she loved to decorate with the thrift store hand me downs she could muster up, and of course she loved buying new stuff for her apartment and gifting her old slightly worn items to whomever she could find that recently signed a lease. She had came along way from the days of her raggedly furniture. When Scooter and Allison grew up and she realized she could have nice things without the stains of food fights. She exercise her desire to live clean and sit on fluffy comfortable furniture was a now a reality for her.

Before I could drag my trash bags of clothes down Myras steps, Sabra was there with boxes of curtains, dishes and pots and pans. Myra wanted me gone so bad she tried to give me the meat out of her freezer. I declined. I was not going to cook it any way. The pots and pans would stay in boxes for many months to come. Instead of getting a curtain rod, and actually hanging the curtains. I just tacked them over the two windows that I had. Getting a couch up those steps was nothing short of a disaster but with help from my friends two blocks over from the fellowship home I had been banned from. We got it. 128 S. Merrill Street would be my home for many years to come. Straight up the stairs and to the right. No washer and dryer hook up gave me great reason not to do laundry often. Lugging groceries up those stairs gave me good reason to eat mostly fast food. The post Civil War era building still looked as it did back in the twenties and few updates to the exterior. My neighbors also wore the depression era looks on their faces. Nobody ever smiling. One always arguing with the other over a drug deal or one would loan another enough foodstamps until their allotment came, then the borrower would refuse to pay back the foodstamps. Always with a junkie move, a sanction from the department, another junkie stole the card. Some of my neighbors had small children which made it worse. Even the little kids did not cast smiling faces.

That building provided nowhere for children to play. So it was not like they could just go outside and ride bikes while their parents smoked up the benefits issued intended on supporting them. The younger children cried most days. The neighbors with the teenagers that was always better than cable. These children would actually fist fight their mothers to run the streets. Gosh don't they know those actions is what got us living like this to begin with. News station coverage was a weekly thing at our building. A story airing about a run away or a shooting or a grown missing person. The stairwell smelled of the detox of local junkies. The only positive thing about Merrill Street was it was pest and rodent free. Jewel said that was only because "even roaches wouldn't live in that building." She is so down to earth yet stuck up at times. I had my own place to stay and I could afford the rent and I was able to walk to work. I did not let her petty comment get to me.

Being as though, I was so close to the fellowship home and Babs has a soft heart I was eventually allowed to reenter. I had to follow gradual rules. At first I could sit only on the porch, as long as I did not cuss out loud or start any fights, or meddle in anyone else's fights, I could sit outside amongst my tribe. When those cold Appalachian winters hit with the fierceness of a ninja sword Babs finally allowed me into the living room. I was still banned from the meetings. I eavesdropped as one addict after another went over their steps, and faced their addiction problems. I found out that Sterling and Phylis had been split up. I knew I could not approach him because Babs may think that I was attempting to start something. He may still be a tad bit frightened of me. On an usually warm winter day I decided to shoot my shot. I decided without giving it much thought, without consulting with my friends and family about what to do. I just acted on impulse. I leaned against the side of a deep red Impala. That just happened to belong to Sterling. Every stride he made closer to his car got me more nervous. Butterflies fluttered, anxiousness and fear made my palms sweat. I was proud of myself for keeping my cool. I did not say or do anything uncouth. I kept my mouth shut and my smile wide. "Would you like to go get something to eat?" I jumped to the passenger side of the car without even giving him an answer. We talked as if we were best friends while he drove. We spent two hours at the Chinese Buffet, eating and chatting. I really wanted him to come upstairs, but he declined by kissing me. The most passionate kiss I have ever had. His body was so close to mine I could smell his cologne on my shirt the next day.

I thought, with my excitement I would not be able to sleep but, that was incorrect. Maybe, just maybe, I do not even know myself. I can not remember a time I slept so soundly. My dreams ignored the dramatics of the street below. He treated me like a lady. I desire to be treated like that all of the time. As always if we have an unusually warm day, the next day is below freezing and snow shaking from the sky. The cold weather tends to keep my neighbors away from fighting amongst each other. Nothing on the street but distant footprints in the blanket of whiteness. I will be dredging in this weather. Unlike my neighbors I can not stay warm inside. I have to work. Shortly after, I moved in this apartment, I landed a job as a telemarketer. That same building only a different company. It is a twenty minute walk. I will be there and I will be on time.

During my walk while the wind stabs my face, the pain radiates through my body from the wind. I watch four wheel drives slide and move slowly in low gear. They all look so warm. I daydream about the winters I have read and heard about down south. I hear that when they get snow even just a flurry the whole state closes. I wish it were like that here. The cold wetness of the snow soaks my knees, but I tread on. I always wanted to live in the south, and bask in that sunshine. I would never leave here because I do not have no support system anywhere but here. You have to be brave to move somewhere, you do not know a soul and just start living. I am not that brave. I will just visit Myrtle Beach every chance I get. It hard to think about sun kisses and salt water in these vicious frigid temperatures. I feel a sense of accomplishment about myself when I make it inside of the building. The heat relieves my aches, although my face and knees still feel as if they are outside.

I make it here on time despite that I walk, despite the weather. This job is very therapeutic for me. I am always dressed like an unmade bed but other than my appearance I never get in trouble with supervisors. They over look my wrinkles and uncombed hair. They know I walk to get here. I enjoy laughing and joking with my co workers during down times. It is if we have a bond. Most of the employees here are people like me. The ones that could not be employed anywhere else. Ones that can only deal with the public behind a screen. Then there are the stellar performers who look at this job as a career. Those are the ones we spend most of the down time laughing at. This is more like a community than a job. That is why I am never late and I give one hundred percent from 8am-4pm Monday – Friday. Jewel, says she worked as a telemarketer once for one month she hated every day of it. I can not understand how someone would not love to do this. She says "It is not for everyone, that is why some people do not do well at it."

CHAPTER THIRTEEN

Four long months has past since our first date. I want him to move

in with me and make it official. He gives a plethora of excuses as to

why he can not. At first it was he needed to get himself together

financially. Now, that he has gave up his house and moved into his

mothers house. He insist he needs to help his sister care for their

mother. I do not understand that. Sally, is a physicians assistant and

his mother gets around better than most people her age. Matter of

fact she has more giddy up than most people my age. I still will not

give up. I still make myself available every Friday night when he

decides he has time for me. I have never had a man to date me the

way he does. He now opens my car door for me, and holds the

umbrella to keep me dry as I remembered watching him do for

Phylis. We go to the movies or to dinner, then he brings me home.

He has still not made his way to the top of the stairs. That leaves me constantly yearning for intimacy. He does not judge my past. Although he is unaware that I still use cocaine every other Friday night when he drops me off.

As soon as his taillights disappear I am wandering the streets if my person does not answer the phone. Luckily my address, keeps me from wandering far. Anything negative here is within arms reach. I would give up my guilty pleasures for Sterling without a doubt. So far I have not had to choose therefore I am not going to do so. I am just as always riding out my life. As always my life is interrupted by my mental illness and horrible events that the game of life tosses at me. Polly, called me. I was at work and missed her call. I knew to return the call because it had to be something important. Since mom has passed away we may have had six phone calls. So I knew to call her back. While waiting on her to answer I anticipated of all of our family whose death she was about to announce. Perhaps one of mom or dads siblings? Maybe my brother was sick? Nothing prepared me for when she answered. "Champ is gone." Champ the child I gave away. Champ who had recently turned twenty one, and had his whole life ahead of him. I did not know anything about him other than he was raised right and worked at a local gas station while he attended college. I knew his eyes were blue and he was the spitting image of his biological father. I could not tell anyone his interest or even what he was majoring in at school. Yet, it felt like the devil ripped my whole heart out.

In the back of my mind I always held on to a fantasy that one day I will be able to at least be friends with my children. Just because I was too selfish, too crazy and too lazy to care for them did not mean that I did not love them. I loved them so much that I gave them away no matter how much people judged me or how it hurt my heart when I woke up the next morning without them. Champ dying so suddenly, made that clear, we will never have lunch together in my older years. Champs heart finally gave out. He had been through numerous surgeries in his life only to borrow a little bit more time here on earth. Times like this I do not know what to do. It is selfish for me to hurt like this, my sister his mother because she raised him. She was there for him since day one. Her hurt has to be amplified versus mine. My only boy will no longer be the target of the church's prayer request. He is with Jesus now. I am angered with God as I pass my neighbors. Why could it not been one of these useless system suckers that God took. Why my only boy? He had a good future ahead of him. Sabra, says "even though it sucks we can not question God." Even if she is right, it makes me wonder how come this has happened? Seems to me if God was so merciful as mom always proclaimed a lot of this suffering in this world. In my mind would not exist. Mom, always had a comeback for that theory. She would speak lessons of choices and accountability. Champ did not choose a bad heart. I did not choose to have my mind interrupted with demonic sounds. I do choose to soothe the demons with drugs. Guilt overtakes my grief. Myra offers words of encouragement letting me know that even if I had raised my son I could not have changed his destiny. That maybe so, however at least I would have known his favorite food.

An overcast sky covers our tiny section of the world as my entire family gets out of their cars wearing hues of dark blue and black. None of Sabras family is in attendance. Not even Jewel. Nobody wants to deal with this side of my family. This side of my family does not want to deal with that side. Once more I feel like the child standing alone in gym class that nobody picked to be on their team. Young faces who most likely graduated with Champ start to fill the church. My first thoughts are these strangers knew my child better than I did. My youngest daughter Ella Mae[i] is here. She is all grown up. She is the opposite of me. Her make up is flawless. It looks professional. Every hair in tact. Mom, would be so proud. I hear Wava, trying to silence her sobs. That breaks my heart. I go and hug her and thank her for all that she has ever done for him, for us, for me. I catch glimpse of my only son laying cold and frozen in a beautiful pearl white box. With his chiseled cheek bones and strong jaw line he . Even in death he spares no resemblance to me. I heard he had my eyes but his eyes are now closed and I can not measure his blue to mine.

Wava's husband Frank, stands at the foot of Champs casket, with a grim look of despair, greeting guest and they flow single file to say their last goodbye. His face tells a story of the possibility that God may have placed more on him than he can bear. I have never seen him so stoic. I feel a tight squeeze from behind. I can not imagine who here wants to hug me. As I turn I see the grinning cheeks of Alisha. My heart is overjoyed. She knew I would have nobody in my corner. She came on my behalf. Moments like this is why I adore her so much. She is a true friend. She is there for me in my darkest times of life. She does not understand my mentality. I do not hold that against her because neither do I. Clumsily, through the crowd we make our way to our seats. My mind drifts away to a place of darkness. Thoughts of his first days on earth while the preacher preaches that Champ has fought a good fight. He mentions the memories of he had of him when he played Joseph in the church play. Wow, I never knew that. I never knew anything and I never let any of it ever bother me.

I hear a buzzing muffled sound of voices. I keep telling myself other people in this church is whispering. Yet, something tells me I am the only one who hears the whispers. It's too hectic and cold inside of here. I have to allow my wails out. I can not run outside like the day we all gathered here to say our goodbyes to mom. Alisha, would kill me and we are sitting dead center pew. This is the point of no return. I have to face this. It hurts my whole soul to hear my sisters cry like that. I wish it were me up there instead of him. The preacher preaches on and I continue to battle wits with God. How is this fair? I am not up there but this sweet boy who fought his whole life for what we take for granted daily. I look away and looking back at me is a reflection of myself. Rhiannon! She has my exact same face only younger. I am in awe. She recognizes me and sends a wide smile to me. The casket closes and the funeral director is gathering the flowers as we pile in lines to exit the church. Alisha, grabs

Rhiannon up and I am afraid she is not going to let go. Alisha's tears

flow like rain off of her cheeks. She holds her tighter. "Gosh, I

missed you so much. I wonder about you every night. You are

beautiful." Rhiannon accepts the hug and turns as if she is waiting

on me to hug her. I do not know what to do. I am pressured and

lean into her embrace. After all I put this girl through she must have

forgiven me. She must love me still. She is the child I liked the least

and abused the most. Polly, rescues me from my discomfort. "Hello,

Alisha my its been a long time you haven't changed a bit. Not a bit."

Polly, did not mean that as a compliment but we decided this was

Champs day and we would accept the compliment. "I am sorry, but

I can not go to the cemetery. I am too weak and I can not take

that." I was disappointed but I understood. I did not want to go to

that creepy place either. "Muffy, you ride with me." Polly said.

I climb into her large SUV. Pollys car is literally nicer than my living

room. A yankee candle air freshener hangs from the rear view

mirror to fill the air with the scent of fresh linen. I should not expect anything less from Polly. The air blowing through the vents feels like it is kissing my skin. Polly eyes stare at me like she is disturbed. "Muffy…." She pauses mid sentence to make sure she has my full attention. "I have to talk to you about Rhiannon." "Okay, I am listening, is she going away to some out of state college or something. Is she going to be a nurse. Ya know she has that look." I respond. "No, I wish, but none of those things will be happening for her. You realize we have done all that we possibly could for her, but she has IT." She spoke as if she was referring the scary killer clown from a Stephen King novel. It took a second for me to process the it she was talking about. My eyebrows raise in astonishment. I split, from my composure and let God know how I was feeling at this second. A very agitated Polly, turns to me and says "This is why, we can not have you around. These outburst makes things worse never better." Her words marinate with me. I would rather her be beside her brother than have It. "How do you know she has It?" I ask. "She has been diagnosed by a doctor. She was making bad impulse decisions, she turned violent on me. We had no choice but to put her out. State agencies will not help place her anywhere because she is not a drug addict. Muffy, we are at the end. I am old now."

I gulp my pride down. "Well at least you don't look old." Polly shrugs and continues down winding paved roads with nothing but mountains in site. We bounce off ideas from each other about how to help Rhiannon. As soon as I think I have come up with a somewhat decent idea, she cuts me off mid sentence. "She is pregnant. The father wants nothing to do with her or the baby. Shocker huh?" Now, I know I can not help in any way. I could not even care for my own children. "Muffy, I can not raise another child. I have her son and after I had to forcibly remove her from our home. I am raising him alone. Sure, my son and daughter help me tremendously but they have their own careers. They are young." Polly starts to sob. She pulls over so she can pull herself together. Her suffering rolls from her eyes until she can not cry anymore. I imagine what this day must be like for her. I feel like I am watching it on a television screen. Today, she burys a nephew and accepts the living death of the daughter she once raised. Polly, and Wava were always so tight. Their children close in age. The children of mine they raised also close in age. Champ is more closer to her like a son than a nephew. She does not even have a day to grieve his loss because of the dramatics with Rhiannon.

How come no cemetery is ever on flat ground? Even in the movies, always on a hill. Wava, has a husband on one arm and a son on the other keeping her from falling to knees as they lower Champs casket into the ground. All of the years, she gave up her life for this baby. All of the doctor appointments and hospital visits just went into the ground. All of the love went with him. He is a memory for her. The best insurance, the best house on the street, and the best parents any kid could ask for still could not save him. I see mom and dads grave sitting beside of his and I wish we were all together again. I wish I could say or do something to comfort someone but I say nothing as a million thoughts bounce like ping pong balls inside of my head.

While waiting on Polly to walk back to the truck, I seen Rhiannon in a distance. She has my walk. My awkward steps. My bull in a china shop poise. I know exactly what life has in store for her. I know the chance the medicine will be hard to calibrate. I wonder how she deals with the scary sounds if the room is too quiet or too loud. I need to get high to escape these thoughts. I need my face and brain to be numb. I can not control anybody's outcome not even my own. I am helpless and it makes me feel like the most useless human being on the planet. On the way, back home I promise Polly, that I am going to step up. My promises are more than likely empty. It sounds like the right thing to say. I continue on, lying about how I have not touched a drug in years. I tell Polly, all about Sterling. She is impressed that he has no criminal record. She credits the Lord for answering their prayers concerning me.

Polly is the epitome of beauty from ashes. For thirty five years she dedicated her life to her home and family. Her one level brick home sits in the curve of a cul de sac. Throughout the years she has added on making that one level home beautiful. Her husband, Mark made his hobby a career. He became a contractor and project manager. Being married to my beautiful sister changed his whole life. Mark, had grew up striving to overcome the alcoholic redneck DNA he was raised with. The only son that had never been arrested. The only son who could drink a beer on the weekends in his own home. Their anniversary celebrations were epic family events. On their twenty fifth one they renewed their vows. Polly was still able to wear the same dress she wore when she first vowed to love him for better or for worse.

He built my sister a house and she gave him a home. She gave him something to be proud of. Thirty five years of marriage stopped mattering to Mark. He must have hated going home to a spotless house and beautiful wife and bragging on his college educated children. Rhiannon seemed to be the only problem their marriage ever had. Previously Mark, had fell and broke his knee at work. He took the pain pills as prescribed. When his prescription ended he began to find pills on the streets. Being as though his family were all still caught up in mud dwellings of white trash, he did not have far to go to fullfill his needs. He gave up on everything he had worked for and left my sister for another woman. She was the total opposite of Polly, instead of working part time and devoting her life to her children and the church. Terri Sue had long since lost her children in the webs of child protective service. She devoted her life to selling drugs to stay high. Terri Sue, never had to worry about the judgement of her family and neighbors because they all participated in the same scandalous dealings.

Terri Sue, with her manly stature and long stringy hair did nothing all day but drink and get high. Mark, felt like he would test to see if the grass was greener on the other side. Living in a dilapidated trailer with no underpinning. Although he possessed the skills to transform that trailer into a house. He lacked the desire. He had found himself content with a constant beer and constant high. He lasted a year in those circumstances before he passed away. Jewel can be so mean her opinion was "He died of natural causes." I explained to her "No, he died of a drug overdose." She said "Yeah, it should be natural to know when you allow someone to shoot heroin in your veins. Then you should naturally know you are going to die." We laughed at her meanness.

This raggedy sofa that hugs my hips is far from comfortable. For some reason the springs scratching my bare legs does not seem to bother me. I continue delving into this True Blood novel as I wait on Sterling to call. He has normally called by this time. It makes it difficult to concentrate on Sookie Stackhouse. My thoughts obsess over him when I am not with him. I wonder what is he doing. Mainly, I wonder who is he doing it with? It makes me want to fight. I am constantly feeling as though I have to compete with other women who are seeking his attention. Jewel, tells me "That is insane, it is not as if he is an Adonis." But he is to me. I intend on keeping him for me.

Months have since passed since Champs funeral. I have not done one thing I promised Polly I would do. Each day revolves around me and me making sure Sterling does not forget about me. Summer is approaching and I really need to feel the wind from the ocean hug my slightly sunburned face. I need to splash in the saltwater and dream about being in the far out waters. It always looks so peaceful out there. Sea creatures swimming in their habitat. Being where they belong. I am always envious of the sharks, and even the mermaids. They just were born where they fit. Unlike me. I have lived my whole life searching for acceptance. Not a day in my life has ever passed that I did not want to be someone else.

I jump up to find my phone, knocking the true blood book in the floor along with my half of glass of Dr.Pepper. I use one of the shirts wadded up on the arm of the chair to dab up the spill. My glasses fall off of my face. I begin to cuss while the phone is still ringing. I cuss with every breath and every step. Even after I hear Sterlings voice, I can not seem to calm myself down. "Muffy! What is wrong? Calm down. Tell me what is wrong?" I can not bring myself to tell him all of my panic is coming from me not wanting to bend down. I start to cry. "Muffy, I am on my way!" What a disaster I just caused. I am always getting myself into messes. He is about to come and see my dirty apartment. I spend the next five minutes, hustling to clear the coffee table only to notice my kitchen trash can is flowing over. I have decided I will just grab a clean tshirt and be at the bottom of the stairs by the time he pulls up.

While on the street, junkies buzz past me. One even ask me for a cigarette. "Get a job, you low life." I rant on about how I do not smoke. How he should not either since he can not afford his habit. My heart suddenly feels a senses of happiness as I see his headlights turn the corner. He can barely put the car in park before I am already sitting beside of him in the passenger seat. He leans into my face and kisses me. This is the best moment of my life. He

has kissed me before but never with this kind of passion. Never

with that much feeling. "Muffy, I missed you today, and I been

thinking..." after a brief pause. He changes the whole direction of

the conversation. "Do you want to go get something to eat?" I am

not even hungry but I fear if I say no he will want to leave so I

accept the invite.

We are back the place we had our first date. I guzzle down an ice

cold Dr. Pepper. When he comes back to the table he grabs my

hand and looks me in my eyes, complimenting me on my skin tone

and brightness of my eyes. I am melting like an ice cube in a cup of

coffee. I know my face is glowing like an alcoholic on New Years

Eve. He smiles back at me. He must sense he is making my life

better. This is really all I ever wanted. A person to be an additive to

my chaotic life. I feel a sense of accomplishment. My preserving all

of these years is paying off this very second. Like a secret in a time

capsule I contain this joy. Guzzling, Dr. Pepper number three and he still has my free hand. "Muffy, I am ready. I want to wake up and look at your face every morning. I see a strong woman inside of you. Tonight when you go to your apartment. I am coming with you." Those words have made me so happy I could care less about the mess on the counters or on the floor.

He opens the car door for me and I flop down inside. I no longer have to impress him. He loves me, for me. I anticipate the first thing we will do when we get inside of the apartment. I am ecstatic. The dim light flickers as we make our way one step at a time to the rest of our lives together. I have ruined this romantic moment. I huff and puff as I ravage through my pockets fumbling for my keys. "Calm down. It's really okay. Just take a minute." Another junkie staggers passed us. "I want to get in to get away from these people." I shout. "Muffy, we are these people." In agreement I say. "I suppose so, I tend to forget that while I am walking to work in the snow while they are still asleep." He chuckles and I open the door. I am ready for him to take me into his arms. His reaction is not at all what I expected it to be. "What's that smell?" He says. I do not smell

anything rancid. Maybe, I am just used to it and I do not realize it

stinks in here. He claims he smells a moldy stench and last weeks

trash. Shows, what he knows. It has actually been weeks since I

have taken out the trash.

"Muffy, we have to clean up a bit. Come on, lets go." We drive five

minutes away to the Dollar General with six minutes before they

close. He grabs a cart like it is noon and he is planning on spending a

lot of time and money in here. He snatches almost every cleaning

supply he can tossing in the cart and racing to the front of the store.

The clerk seems annoyed that we are holding her up from leaving. I

do not say anything because I do not want to show my fit of rage in

front of Sterling. I make a mental note to come back this time

tomorrow night all by myself so I can cuss her out like she deserves.

I go into explaining how I got sick and could not clean as I normally

do. I work long hours and walk each way so I am too tired when I

come home. This time when I open the door. I see my apartment from his perspective. Wrinkled clothes some washed some unwashed. Some still damp clutter the couch. A tiny wet puddle by my chair from where I spilled the Dr. Pepper earlier still lingers. The kitchen counter is full of empty fast food bags and half eaten sandwiches. 32oz styrofoam cups laying in every direction on each end of the side tables. Ashamed. What would I do if my aunt Myra saw how I was living without her caring for me?

"Muffy, help me gather this trash up, and I will take it downstairs. It is no wonder in this neighborhood why you do not want to take your trash out at night. We are going to clean it spic and span then in the morning I am going to take you to work." I bounce cups and other trash in the bag and stay in unison with him as he makes every plausible excuse for my filth. I even lie and tell him that I will clean everyday as long as he never leaves my side. He assures me that he is here to stay.

I was able to just reach over and grab my glasses this morning without the stress of knocking trash in the floor or the stress of not being able to find them. I love how it smells like bleach and pine sol. It reminds me of being at Myras. I love how I can just look down and see the On the way to the shower I did not stumble over piles of clothes. Sterling knows what is best for me. That is why last night I cowered down and joined him in this cleaning endeavor. Instead of cussing him out like I felt like doing. I wanted to brag to my friends and family about how he cleaned my whole apartment up. I was too ashamed to admit to them that my apartment needed it that bad.

CHAPTER FOURTEEN

I called Sabra on my lunch break to tell her all about my new love life. Her negative comments discouraged me. "Muffy, that man wont stay with you when he sees how nasty you live. He will leave you for the first thing that smiles back at him, the first time you throw a tantrum in public. The first time you start screaming for no reason... he is gone." I can never figure Sabra out. For years she has advised me on how I can get this man to love me. Then once I have accomplished my goal. She is negative. She continued on to say "Do not let that man move in with you, if you do he will never marry you." I am not looking for a husband. I do not care about his future intentions. I live for the here and now. She raises questions until I become frustrated and cuss her like the hateful dog she is. "Wonder, what happened to make him move in with you after all of this time? What? Has he been put out? Back on that dope? Or maybe he knows you got that HUD certificate and does not want to pay rent?" She basically said, no man can ever love me for me. I cussed her and slammed the phone, adding another crack to my screen.

Her negative, outlook on me, has planted a seed of worthlessness in me. Jewel, always comes to Sabras defense. "Muffy, after the men we have chose in our life, Sabra is only on guard. I am sure everything with Sterling will be fine. Sabra's job as an older woman is too guide us with wisdom." She did agree that she could have been more subtle. We both know that trait does not exist in Sabra. I still desire to talk to Allison, about the topics that me and Alisha or Jewel have. Anytime I call her she says "I do not have time for all that conversation right now, So how much money do you got? What time can you be here?" Her drug use has worsened over the years. I am bad, I will spend every cent to my name and not think about how will I have money for food. As long as I have money, and I am high. I do not worry with how I will pay my phone or power bills.

Allison, used to function and work and still maintain while getting high. Something happened along the way she got caught up. She is so entangled that any dime she gets she spends on drugs. She got fired from a job she had worked for years. She wanted to stay up all night and party then could not wake up to get to work at time. Losing that job took her sense of pride away and made her habit worse. She now works as a professional shop lifter to supply her habit. Jewel, did the math on that. She estimated that Allison, makes approximately four hundred fifty dollars a day. At least five days a week. Allison, looks at this as if it were a career. Jewel, said "Well, making that kind of money, she should." It gives me some kind of winning spirit to know that my habit is not as bad as hers. Alisha, sits back and laughs and judges us all. Still to date, she does not have much material assets. On the other hand she does not have any felony convictions either.

My whole life has been as if I have lived in a tornado. Just twisting and spinning, with no direction or destination in site. Wherever I land it ends up a destroyed disaster. Same mistakes. Same results. For whatever reason, I am always surprised with the results. I feel like if I abuse myself what gives anyone reason to mistreat me. Yet, they still do. Life is not fair like Myra always says. If I were born with beauty I think my life would have been different. At least if I had not have been born with these demons bouncing in my head I know my life would be different. Polly referred to our schizoaffective disorder as IT. I have to refer to IT as THIS. Truthfully, THIS is worse than a scary clown chasing children around some Massachusetts town. THIS never ends unless I am high on cocaine. I admit with Sterling being in the apartment I am able to ignore spontaneous whispers. I am able to distinguish different tones in my head. My mood is never depressed unless I talk with Sabra.

Sterling swept me off of my feet and keeps me grounded. He takes care of everything. He does fuss about my messiness at times. He does it with a lighthearted jokingly spirit. He even holds my bank card to make sure that I can stay clean, sober and do not squander my money away. It is like he read my mind all of those years I spent reading him. He wants us to save for a house with a nice yard. He is the first man I have ever had that gives me quality time and plans

for our future together. I have never followed through on a plan my

entire life. I know all will be fine. He has our best interest in mind.

In the mornings he spends one hour meditating while I am sleeping.

He does not want me to cook meals for him anymore. He learned

the hard way it should be a felony for me to own a stove. He

implied that I am too lazy to follow a recipe. He does all of the

cooking. Most of what he cooks is either dry or bland. The flavor is

missing. It does not taste gross it just takes like nothing. At least

what he prepares is not burnt to a crisp or raw like when I cook. I

am grateful while I chew wishing it was something Myra had

cooked.

Sterling, makes sure that I am growing into a better person. He

marches to a a beat of a different drum. His family name is

prominent amongst local republican leaders. He grew up hob

knobbing in the state capitol. Conservative values? Is that even a

thing? I know nothing about political science all of that is not exciting enough to capture my attention for a minute. I go about political views with common sense. No matter who is elected in office the lives of me and my family does not change one bit. Sterling views favor a democratic point. They actually have a family rule no discussing politics at the family gatherings. I met his mother and two of his sisters. I was so nervous of what to wear and how to act. He coached me before we went inside. "Do not drop the F-bomb or the G-D! And you will be fine." I expected to see a picture perfect family. An old colonial style home that possibly one time served as a dwelling for a master and his family. Massive large columns, a spiral stair case, hardwood floors casting our reflections on the floor. Their home has all of the features a Better Homes and Gardens magazine. My preconceived notions led me to believe the residents of this home were going to be One Life to Live cast replicas. Once more I was wrong. His physicians assistant sister appeared to care about the health of others than she does her own. Her chubby hands was hugging a 20 ounce Mt. Dew. She was still wearing her scrub top. Bags under her eyes showed she spends a lot of sleepless nights. A stacked bob hatted her head apparently

weighted down with two cans of hairspray. Not one strand of hair

out of place. Her hair did not even move when she bent down. Her

turtle neck of chins did not take away from her beauty. Squared

pearls between her lips. I have never seen teeth as pretty. Her deep

dimples seemed to chuckle every time she smiled. I expected a

woman with her status would only have conversations with topics

of intellect.

She has a dry sense of humor. An old maid. She has never lived

outside of her mothers site. His other sister Leah, wore the wrinkles

of alcoholism better than anyone I have ever saw. Her body is a

trophy of how many plastic surgeons children, she has put through

college. Nothing real except her skin and even that has been

tucked. She slurred her speech a little bit. They all assured their

mother Leah is slurring from the side effect from the stroke she had

years ago. I giggled inside a bit. Leah, took her inheritance from her

fathers death and invested some money into a few stocks. That luckily for her skyrocketed. She graduated college with a masters degree in finance. She is better with money drunk than most people I know sober. She moved to a tiny house somewhere in the Cayman Islands. She flies back home once a year. The gossiped about how she ruins the whole visit by fussing about how cold it is here. I did not speak my mind but I thought her drinking was disrespectful to Sterlings recovery. He is the only boy and no matter his sisters accomplishments, he is still favored by their mother.

I felt intimidated by the level of degrees as his cousins wandered in. In fear of saying something stupid I remained quiet and clammed up. Sterling dropped out of college his junior year. I do not know if his former drug addicted lifestyle or because he votes democrat is why they have deemed him the black sheep. I could not sense any maltreatment. When we left he assured me that is was there. It was almost two decades ago when he let go of his addiction. I feel like if he can let go of his demons they should let his demons go as well. I asked him on the way home "Are you embarrassed to live where we do?" His response should be published in a book on recovery.

"As long as I am sober and doing what I am supposed to do to be a better person than the day before, I am not ashamed." He is always so insightful.

As time passed by everything was beginning to fall into place for me. Life became worth living. Sterling handles all of the bills so I have not had to worry about falling behind on payment arrangements with the power company, or arguing with the landlord over the eighty five dollar portion of my rent that I owe. HUD only allots me four hundred dollars a month for rent. I look forward to seeing him come home after work. We spend quiet nights reading until we are sleepy or disturbed by the violence on the streets.

I was not given the option to not follow through with my promise to Polly about Rhiannon. Sterling is too good of a person to let me allow my own daughter to sleep on the streets, especially due to give birth any day. Rhiannon refuses to take her Geodon while pregnant. She is scared of harming the baby. Polly, is afraid she is going to harm herself or others. Polly, was successful with the courts in getting a restraining order against Rhi-Rhi. Polly, had locked her out of the house after she stole a few items from her jewelry box. Rhi-Rhi, then busted the living room window out and came inside of the house. Polly, went on to say that Rhi-Rhi took the sliced cheese from the refrigerator and placed it in the shape of the figure 8 in the kitchen floor. She then went and got in her bed and laid down as if all of that was okay.

Rhi-Rhi, has been staying with us for the past two weeks and I am losing my whole mind. Her whiny high pitched voice sounds like nails on a chalkboard. I will do everything in my power to help her because Sterling will think bad of me if I do not. Her messy habits annoy me. I do not like picking up after myself much less another person. She wanders around the apartment all day while we work. To get peace of my mind and quiet time I give her a few dollars and let her walk to the store to get cigarettes and snacks. I secretly hope she does not find her way back here. Much to my disappointment she does. Is it cruel of me not love her the way a mother is supposed love her daughter? I was unable to bond with her and share childhood memories. Even though we are still under the same roof we are still distant. I care for her. That is the extent of it.

We bicker sounding like me and Allison. It is starting to bear stressful weight on Sterling. He is ready to pay a deposit for whatever apartment she can find. She does not attempt any stealing or violent nature here, because she knows I will kill her and just be in prison for the rest of my life. I do not keep my hostility a secret. I try to talk to her about how she can not stay here forever. I am resentful, that she is even here. I was not allowed to take my crazy antics to Sabras house and impose on her. It irks my nerves when she scoots her feet across the floor as if she is too lazy to pick her feet up and take a step. She constantly talks to herself or perhaps she is communicating with the voices in her mind. Sterling treats her as she is his daughter. He makes sure she gets to all of her prenatal appointments. We even take her to her psychiatrist appointments. I see a slew of my old friends from my bar days in the waiting room. Each appointment is a new reunion for me.

Rhi-Rhi's pregnancy is not the only thing that separates her looks from the other people in the lobby. She is the youngest face there each time. She still possesses her youthful looks. By appearance you can not see the illness that plagues her mind. She looks healthy as a horse. She even carries her pregnancy as if she is built for breeding. She has suffered no morning sickness, no swelling. Just happy go lucky this whole time. Sterling said I should finally start feeling good about myself since I am trying to correct my past mistakes. That even makes me feel worse. I am only doing this because he would know that I am really a rotten person. Sabra, said I am incapable of fixing her because she can not be fixed. She implied that I am not her mother and since Polly, was so diligent in keeping her away from us all of these years that Polly, should continue that same pattern. Sabra, is adamant about standing strong on her beliefs that THIS what we have did not come from her side of the family. She reassures me that the Watsons are environmentally crazy because we have to be.

I wish that I had it in my heart to brag on Rhi-Rhis blonde curly tresses, her IQ and flawless skin. I also wish that Sabra would welcome her with open arms. I know the whole time we are there I have to keep my eyes on Rhi-Rhi, in case she steals something. Sabra would absolutely beat her and me half to death. Rhi-Rhi was welcomed by Allison. Allison begged Sabra to let her keep her as if she were a stray kitten. Jewels evil husband, was out of state tucked under the earth in some coal mine. So Allison, took Rhi-Rhi to Jewels house. That lasted about six days. Jewel was sitting in her recliner rocking and watching television when Rhi-Rhi jumped to her feet, she ran to the bedroom and was yelling for Allison. Allison runs behind her. Gasping for breath she said. "You got to help me get rid of them! I need a knife and your help." Allison, asked her

"What the hell do you mean? What are you talking about?" " Look this is serious business, if you do not help me I will have to do it all by myself, it has to be done."Rhi-Rhi, still in a panic said. "Oh my your ass is too crazy ain't ya." Allison said.

While Jewels dark shoulder length hair bounced as she rocked. That song Witchy Woman by the Eagles started playing in Rhi-Rhis mind. She got it in her mind that Jewel was a bad witch because of her dark hair and she must be killed or she was going to kill her. That was the only explainable excuse Allison could get from her. She immediately took Rhi-Rhi to another friends house and kept rotating her from house to house. No matter how humble or how rough her friends were not one single of them could keep Rhi-Rhi. Nobody could deal with the crazy. She told Allison, about when she had been homeless before her pregnancy. How people from the streets made fun of her. How she would have to sleep with men for a place to stay and sometimes they would put her out anyway. She even told her this story about this apartment in the projects where she ended up and how they told her they was giving her cocaine but it was Tide washing powder she was really snorting. Those women in that house laughed contagiously at how sick she got.

It just so happened to be their luck that Allison, knew those girls and knew them well. Worse of all they knew Allison. There was not one woman who laughed at Rhi-Rhi that wanted to fight Allison. She told them since they like laughing so much how would they like if she laughed while she stomped their rib cage through their backs. Suddenly they did not find no humor in their cruel prank. They just pointed their fingers at each other. Refusing to take responsibility, none stepping up to the fight Allison offered. I will be the first to admit I do not love her like a mother should, but I will be damned if I allow anyone abuse her. Sterling knew if we did not invite her to stay in our tiny one bedroom apartment she would be giving birth in a dumpster. 320 million people in this country and she ends up on my couch.

CHAPTER FIFTEEN

And, soon there were four of us cooped up like refugees. Following

an unwritten generational clause. Just as Stevies mother did, and

Stevie did, and Sabra did and I did and Rhi-Rhi did the eldest girl

child would be born in the month of April. April brings us Easter,

Spring break, snowstorms and birthdays. None have ever touched

my heart like when I laid eyes on this heavenly ham. Holly Pearl has

changed my whole aspect on life. Finally, I desire to be a better

person. No gift could be greater than when that little baby grabbed

my finger. I know how Sabra feels. These babies have no clue

grasping your finger will their chubby fingers is stealing your heart

for eternity. It is an amazing feeling. My excitement showed through my tears. Holly Pearl evoked emotions that I have never witnessed in a man. After Sterling gleamed with joy from holding her. He passed her back to Rhi-Rhi. I looked around the corner of the hospital room. I. noticed he was kneeling. At first glance I thought perhaps he had dropped something. He was down on his knees too long. He raises up and takes his glasses off and wipes his cheeks and eyes. I asked him "What were you doing?" He replied "Praying..."

Up to that point, Sterling believed in a higher power. It is a recovery requirement. But it was never God. He was atheist. He always insisted that religious people are weak minded, people who can not rely on theirselves so they look to Jesus or other forms of religions for help. He was too involved in the evolution theory and facts he claimed proved it was not a theory it was a fact. Having such a close encounter with the glorious power of Jesus during childbirth. He had changed his mind. We were in the room with her. Sabra, claimed it was weird, that a man would want to go into a labor and delivery room with someone who was not his wife. She may

sometimes hit the nail on the head but this time I knew she was off

on the hit. Sterling did not have a choice to decline to go inside.

Sterling was driving us to another lengthy psychiatrist appointment.

Traffic, was abnormally heavy that morning of April 20th. Fog was

casted over the mountains. The news reported only a five feet

visibility. I begged them to cancel the appointment, just reschedule

for a later prettier day. But Sterling, insisted that it was rude to

cancel the day of an appointment and since he took a personal day

to make sure that she got to the appointment. He was not

interested in missing another day of work for the same task that

could just be handled today. So off we go me cussing the whole way

to the car. I even told Rhi-Rhi I wish I had of aborted her when I had

the chance. The tension in the car was thicker than the fog.

Rhi-Rhi, screamed out. I ignored it thinking that she was cooing for

attention. Another scream of terror and I had gave birth enough to know that the sound was not for attention. The backseat sloshed when her water broke. A coal truck, in front of us. He couldn't get around. He used the edge of the road to pass the traffic. Full speed and hazard lights blinking. The twenty minute drive to the hospital was made in seven minutes. I didn't wait for the car to get fully stopped before I jumped out running into the ER. It took seconds to for nurses to come to the car for her. Sterling had stepped out sweating in the cold. His sensors were in panic. He needed air. He walked to the back of the car to help them get her into the wheelchair as I was still slowly walking back to the car. They insisted that he come up with them. He was shocked to a passive state.

I seen him aiding them with her and shouted for the keys. I will park and be right up there. Holly Pearl, was born in the elevator while I drove around the parking lot six times looking for a place to park. We had never had the discussion on anything pertaining to the delivery and who would go into the delivery room with her. We did not even have anything for the baby. But all of that would change when Holly Pearl came. When we left the hospital we went baby shopping. We held hands and picked out everything pink we could find. Best day of my life by far. I called fifty people to tell them I had a grand doll. If I had demons in my mind on that day, the joy in my heart subsided them. That night Sterling fell asleep with the Bible on his chest. I questioned God and anybody else that would listen about why did I not feel this overjoyed when I had my own children? It would be Allison, out of everyone who would deliver me the blunt brutal honesty with an accurate answer. "You are a crazy as all of hell." We laughed at her accuracy.

If Holly Pearl sheds a tear, I want to do everything in my power to comfort her. I want to make her life better. I cry and beg God every single night "Please, God don't cast our demons on her. Please, make her smart and thank him for her physical health." I want the best possible life for her. Sterling is putty in her hands. He cradles her as he rocks her to sleep. A gentle giant. He changes her like it is nothing. Most men whine or complain, if they have to change a dirty diaper. He has no choice. My stomach still churns at the stench

of a dirty diaper. It is as if me and Sabra repeat the same

conversations from decades ago. She used to tell me "Why does

diapers bother you so bad? Knowing the way you live and keep

house." Same exact words she told me back when my kids were

babies.

Rhi-Rhi, found her an apartment. Ten stories of poverty. Dissolved

hopes and dreams congregating on the front steps by the door as if

they are potted plants. People with the least in life, laughing the

most. Rhi-Rhis was fortunate to get on the second floor. Across the

hall was a tiny lady with too many stories to tell. She also had a lot

of opinions to give. She often checked in on Rhi-Rhi. Cigarette and

coffee trading is a constant morning routine amongst the neighbors

who live there. There are so many similarities between us. Perhaps

that is why I can not stand her most of the time. Everything, I hate

in myself I see in her. Sterling and me visit as much as possible. I

rarely, ever hear him use foul language. Until we are visiting. He spends little time cuddling with Holly Pearl, and most of the time cleaning. Cussing under every breath. Just as my dad used to do for me.

I hold her and feed her. She coos while I tell her my dreams as if she understands what I am saying. Her chubby cheeks bounce as I rock her. Sterling leans down and gives her kisses. He shows his love in other ways like buying formula because Rhi-Rhi forgets to go to her WIC appointments or trades the formula for a few packs of cigarettes. Sterling told her that he would rather buy cigarettes than formula. "Enfamil is more expensive than cancer sticks." He buys all of the diapers and clothes just as my parents did for me when I had her. I am watching history repeat itself but I can not confide into Sterling. I admitted to him "I suck as a mother." It is not my fault that attributed my bad parenting skills to an addiction. An addiction I did not have back then. It is no need to get into all of that small talk. The results were the same regardless.

I strive to make good choices so that I can give this baby a good life. I want her to have everything we did not. Parents, and grandparents that get a long well. Positivity. Most importantly, sanity. All babies look to the ceiling and laugh, sometimes they cry. It terrifies me as an infant she maybe seeing things that are not there, like me and her mother do. The baby books reassure me that it is just the baby learning to focus. Sterling has read every book from Dr. Spock to Dr. Seuss. He has never even been around small children. He told him that Holly Pearl, makes him feel stupid. "As tiny as she is how can she intimidate me so fiercely." He bought her a pink wooden sign that read Tiny But Fierce. He is a good man even better one when he is caring for our grand doll.

CHAPTER SIXTEEN

There is more happiness, more to live for despite the chaos that surrounds our days. Rhi-Rhi, had a moment of terror. She swaddled my grand doll up and ran for her life. She knew she had to keep the baby safe no matter how many hills she had to run up. She ran to Jewels panting. "Please, let me in you have to help. Those women on the corner were laughing at me. They wanted to fight me. They were yelling! They said they were going to call child protective services on me." Jewel said she collapsed in her arms begging her to help. Jewel, went outside, to find the women Rhi, was referring to. She knew there was no chance she would see anyone gathered in a group in her neighborhood. She checked because, in her words. "You never know." The search was a bust nothing but crickets chirping.

No doubt in Jewels mind Rhi-Rhi believed what she heard and saw to be real. Jewel said her screams were so intense it made the hair on her nape of her neck stand up. Jewel reached out to cuddle Holly Pearl. I would like say all was well by the time we got there. Holly

Pearl, hates Jewel. Only a few people in this world hate Jewel and my grand doll is one of them. Maybe, it is the smell of Newport's and caramel coffee creamer that make her smell like pancake syrup. Holly Pearl, is likely to sense the wicked streak Jewel has too. She can go from zero to two hundred in a second. She would never hurt any child or anybody who did not hurt her first. Jewel spent hours the next day calling shelters, calling mental health clinics, and social workers to get help for Rhi-Rhi to no avail.

She learned the lesson we already knew. Rhi-Rhi is unlikely to get help unless she gets strung out on drugs. She has had her time on the psychiatric wards. She needs long term care. They drug her up. She functions highly, then one day this happens. We took Holly Pearl home with us for the next few days. We had to return back to our jobs. I hated taking that baby home to her in fear she would suffer at the hands of her mentally ill mother like she did as an infant. Babies that age are so vulnerable they can not speak and tell you when they have been harmed. They can not point and show you where anything hurts. I beg God to protect her. She is special.

She has a purpose in this world from the second she was born she

changed lives. Sterling the factual atheist is now praying to God all

mighty. My mom would be so proud I am involved with a praying

man. Shocked to her socks but proud. She changed my life too. She

makes me want to focus on a real life instead of settling for what I

have.

A month passed no outburst, no problems. Peace. Until my phone

starting ringing at two o'clock in the morning. Sadie, the neighbor

from across the hall was so flabbergasted. "Y'all, got to get here

now! She in there arguing with someone it sounds bad. I hear things

breaking. I knocked she wont answer. I do not call police on

nobody. But if you want me to I will." Sterling rolled over grumbling.

His patience growing as thin as his hairline. He flopped and rolled

back over in the precious ambience of his slumber. "NO, please do

not call the police. We will be right there." I push Sterling to wake

him back up. He rolls to his feet. "Let's Go!" That is the Sterling way to go from sleeping to superhero within twenty seconds. A dream of winning the powerball would not have kept Sterling from jumping in that car to go rescue our baby.

I ran up the flight of stairs like a firefighter coming to save the elderly. I could hear the cussing from the floor below. Sterling starts pounding on the door as if he had been trained to knock in the police academy. The voices stop. Silence. "Open this damn door Rhiannon." He shouted. Another sound of glass breaking. Sterling knocks as if the hinges of are coming unloosened. I scream until my voice gets numb. Rhiannon, opens the door. Her face appeared swollen from crying. Her hair frazzled. Her clothes look loose on her. Glass is everywhere on the floor. Holly Pearl was screaming until she was three shades of red and purple. I ran over to that sweet little soul and rocked her. I nestled her tight against me while Sterling searched the whole apartment all closets and under beds. Nothing. Not only were there nobody else in the apartment. No sign that anyone had been there other than the shattered glass on the floor.

I quizzed her until I lost my patience about who she had been arguing with. I really lost my cool. I jumped up in her face. Sterling wedged himself in the middle of us. She stared me down with those soulless eyes. Her nowhere stare was not intimidated by my anger. Sterling used the calm approach to get the answers we drove in the dark to get. Rhi-Rhi looked at him with a naïve sense, she pointed to the ceiling. "Them. They were laughing at me and calling me crazy. But I showed them I will fight." At that moment Sterling realized we were fighting a losing battle. We swaddled our baby once more taking her back to our unsafe neighborhood for safety. He pulled the car over and cried so hard. "God why? Why inflict this on people, especially mothers." The next morning we went back. This time she came with us. She was admitted into the hospital. Sterling and I were parents for the next two weeks. I was in bliss. Each day I felt like I had been given the opportunity to right my wrongs.

I want Sabra, to be proud of me. She has a way of predicting a negative future. Like a bitter meteorologist forecasting gloomy skies bringing blizzards. "Y'all, just wasting your time and getting attached to a baby you wont never see grow up." I debate with her all of the reasons why I will never lose Holly Pearl. She redirects the conversational subject to another negative outlook. "Why does Sterling make decent money and still hold your paycheck from you? If he was saving for a house, he should have had enough by now. Unless he is not working." I explain that he never misses work unless it is an emergency. "Why, does he keep y'all in that neighborhood as bad as it is?" She can be so hasty when I need her to be happy. She went on to examine my business like she is a relevant private investigator. "Hmm, seems to me if someone makes the kind of money he does and still chooses to live there, he's either on drugs or likes to use those that are. It doesn't make sense to me to get off drugs and still live like you use them." She just doesn't understand. Sterling, knows what it best for us. I can not help it she spends all of her money on wastefulness. Eating out, furniture and Jewels kids. Not to mention her other two grown kids she caters to.

I immediately called Jewel after I hung up with her. She always builds me up. She is proud of me and happy God is giving me a second chance to do what is right. Unfortunately, she agrees with Sabra, on why we are still stuck in this apartment building. She said as if they had rehearsed this sentence. "It makes no sense, why a person would get off drugs and still wallow where drug addicts roam, especially if they have a choice." Allison, is full of a bitter heart. She always quizzes me about if I hit Holly Pearl. If I am bathing her regularly. She can not let go of how I parented my own children. She has never given birth so I do not see how it is okay for her to judge me. My mind ponders what makes these women so full of distrust and bitterness. Generation after generation not able to trust people, mostly men. Alisha, is happy for me. She is proud of me. She knows my heart. She respects Sterling for stepping up, no matter our address. I wish my family could, understand like she does. We have to be close in the community. Sterling is very active in the recovery programs. He may have to leave in the middle of the night to be the superhero he is. He needs to be close to help those that are trying to overcome their demons.

Alisha, credits him for me being such a divine grandparent. She thinks that if my own children's fathers would have contributed that I may have been a better mother. If I had help or not I should have did my part towards them. I should have modeled her and the other strong women who have been influences in my life. Alisha, had almost zero help and her oldest daughter is going to medical school next fall. She stays humble when I compliment her on raising such amazing daughters. I never imagined when we were nineteen year old mothers cooped up in the house on cold days we would reach this point in our lives where we found peace. We have. It is going to be alright after all.

Waking up at 2am for feeding and rocking came to an end when Rhi-Rhi was released from the hospital. A human with a mental illness was admitted and a zombie was released. We stopped to get stack of prescriptions filled for her. I hope she does not take them all. One medicine has side effects, then another medicine counteracts the other. Sterling, does not trust that she is cured, or even pacified. We have no choice at this point but to return this sweet bundle of joy to her. It felt like my whole heart had been ripped out watching her carry our baby up the steps. Sterling looked stoic and in fear of what will be next when we have to jump out of bed and rush back over here. With this time of just us, I wanted to ask him if there was any truth to Sabra and Jewels theory. I kept my lips sealed and watched him grieve for a life that is not lost. I did not want to stir up a smoke at a time like this. I just held my thoughts to myself and began overthinking every single time he had been called out in the middle of the night by a sponsee.

Both of our hearts were breaking. Bonding with someone really

stinks. He has no words to comfort me and I have no words to

comfort him. We just ride away with our fears anxiety by what is

left to come. He called an attorney friend of his as soon as we got

home. Jewel, with no legal degree disputed every word Sterlings

friend with a juris doctorate said. It is difficult to talk to her

sometimes. Even Scooter says "It is impossible to talk to someone

who knows everything." He may not be right about a lot of things.

Every blue moon he speaks a truth that a philosopher would envy. I

know nothing about legal matters what so ever. I am smart enough

to trust the person with a degree, who is a friend to Sterling, versus

an unemployed house wife. My IQ should never be questioned. For

some reason the smarter I am on an intelligence level, the more

severe my mental illness is. I hate to rate Jewel in a lower status.

She is truly a hero to me. Facts are facts.

It would not be long before Polly, was to get a call from a child

protective service worker. They were in Rhiannon's apartment, standing in the filth. Looking amazed while she talked to the people in the ceiling, as they waited for the police to come assist them. One of the neighbors in that building offered an anonymous tip. She called me and Sterling first. We both left work and rushed right over there. From where I had lost custody of my children twenty some odd years ago, they still held that against me and would not let me have custody of Holly Pearl. Sterling and me are not married so that excluded him from getting custody. I would have left our apartment in a New York minute if he would have been allowed to leave. I lost it. It had been us from day one who kept this sweet baby in everything she needed. Nine whole months of life we have loved and supported her. Nurturing her each chance we got. Stealing minutes from work to get to her a little bit sooner than later. All for this worker who was too young to even have children to judge me. My foul mouth let go of every word that would have got me banned from a sailors bar. Sterling softly grabbed my waist. The look of ire on his face stabbed me. "Be quiet, I have got this handled already. Let's go." I did not leave silently. I did leave.

Even though it was after hours, he called his attorney friend on his

cell phone and sit up an appointment for the following day. Sterling

gave me, a stern talking to. You might say a come to Jesus meeting.

He warned me not to use cuss words. Not to make any foul jokes

when we met with his friend. It really disturbed me. I may be crazy

and do ludicrous acts from time to time. I know how to behave in

social settings especially something as important as this. A tiny

petite man walked in the waiting room. His lopsided large glasses,

wrinkled white oxford shirt and the blood shot lines circling his blue

irises, gave the impression that he had been overworked the entire

morning. He took the last five hundred dollars to Sterlings name

and said because he is a personal friend he will wait on the rest of

the thirty five hundred dollar retainer fee. He went on to say that

fighting child protective services could be a long process and could

cost up to seventeen thousand dollars by the time it was all said

and done.

He was so thorough in his explanation about the whole process. All that we will go through. All that they will make Rhiannon go through. He even quoted a poet "The greater the power, the more dangerous the abuse." He warned us that keeping Holly Pearl out of states custody and keeping her with family was detrimental to this case. He promised that in the end he would win and our fight would not be for custody because of my not so immaculate past, but we would fight for Grandparents rights. We left the law office feeling at ease. For the first time in nine months we were able to enjoy our lunch, because we did not have to worry about running cigarettes or formula to Rhi-Rhi. That night we slept soundly as if we were on our way to the pearly gates. We knew Polly would be giving our baby the best love and support. She would keep her safe and abided by all of the rules the agency set forth.

The next day, the pain set in. I may not ever be able to hold her again because of my past. I felt like I did not want to get out of bed as if my legs were weighted with cinderblocks. All too real signs that my sickness is coming back. Sterling, is much stronger than me. He

diverted his hurt into doing some extra volunteer work at the food

bank. He relied on hope of the win his friend told us we would be

victorious in. Of course, when I am sad I call Jewel for motivation. I

told her about all the things that attorney friend told us. I

remembered his words to the exact science and even recited them

back to her using the exact same tone. Jewel, paused. "Muffy.." I

interrupt "What." Her serious tone responded. "Muffy, there is no

such of thing as grandparents rights in this state. What is going on?

Why would he tell you y'all could win? Even F. Lee Bailey can not

assure a win. These things are up to a judge. These matters are

handled with court appointed attorneys so they can bill the state

for hours that they have worked and not work. Why would y'all pay

for an attorney when the court will provide one at no charge?

Muffy, I do not like this. When is your next appointment with this

guy?"

"You mean our attorney? It will be as soon as my income tax hit my card." Jewel never would refer to him as an attorney. While, on the phone she researched. She came back with positive feedback from his website and reviews. Other than that, she had no more good words to say about him. By the end of that day she was texting me information. She knew where he went to law school. She knew his gpa in high school, even the crowd of kids he hung out with. She even knew how long he had been in practice. But she did not know why he would charge us for such poor legal advice.

CHAPTER SEVENTEEN

Being as though my heart broke more and more each day. I fought it. I fought it so hard. I wanted to be high and escape my heartache. I knew Sterling was going to account for each cent I spent. I could never play that I lost my bank card if he even parted with it. I took walks. I read books and when I was done I reread the same book. When my income tax refund hit on the card the tax office handed me when I filed my taxes. My demons finally became victorious. I hit the street as if I had a hot scratch off ticket. I was so high I lost all concept of time. For the first time since Sterling and I got together I ignored his phone call. He must have got worried because he called back to back which then made me paranoid that he was going to find out that I was high. I did not answer those calls either. Finally, I came down enough to call him back. He could tell in my voice that I was high. He begged me to come home. I got scared that he was going to do some kind of physical harm to me. I told him I would be home in forty five minutes. I did not make good on my word. The back and forth calling went on until the next morning. By morning I was at Jewels house watching Sterling circle her block looking for me.

He called her, I told her to ignore it. He kept calling finally she answered. She made me talk to him. Sterlings voice was cracking as if he had tears in his throat. "Please, Muffy do not spend no more money this money is for to get our grand doll you know this. Do you not care that she may grow up in a foster home? Is your high more important than Holly?" I broke down, every emotion I had spent 1500 dollars to escape from came back. "Muffy, if you do not want to come home I can not make you. But I want that money card. I do not want you to waste any more money." I went on to tell him "I am scared you are going to hurt me." "Muffy, I am sending Trevor to go get that card from you. Do you still have the money we owe him on it?" We bounced calls back and forth and I agreed to meet his attorney friend at a gas station.

Jewel gave me a ride to meet him. While we waited I took another four hundred dollars off the card. I no more had made it back to her Jeep when a shiny black BMW pulled up behind her. Trevor took short confident strides toward the passenger side of the Jeep. Through the window I handed him the card wrapped in an ATM receipt with the PIN number scribbled on it. He did not speak or say thank you. No words were exchanged. Jewel, lit me up. "What kind

of lawyer picks up a retainer fee at a gas station on a Saturday?"

She yelled. "One that needs thirty two hundred dollars." I replied.

"Muffy, No, please tell me you are joking. He looks like he has been

on a high. Is he a crackhead Sterling knows from those useless

meetings y'all attend?" I did not entertain her questions. "I don't

know, Sterling and him are buddies that is all I know. I can not do

anything about it, we are desperate to get custody of Holly Pearl."

Sterling did not dial my number another time. He was disappointed

in my actions. I was glad about it because I was able to enjoy my

high. Four hundred dollars did not last me long. I returned home

Sunday night to a man who had lost all faith in me. I felt so guilty, so

ashamed. He stewed in his anger for days not speaking to me. I

would rather him have punched me or cussed me than give me the

silent treatment.

Life resumed back to normal. Sterling never let me forget my

mistake. We dealt with it. We also found out that the battle with the department was bigger than we ever imagined. Rhi-Rhi was assigned a new case worker. An overweight man who looked as if he was a retired truck driver. His khaki slacks appeared to come out of my laundry basket. He adored Rhiannon. He was an advocate for her. When Polly called to inform us that her new worker was going to recommend she get full custody back. It sounded too good to be true. We all showed up for the court date. "Your honor, there is no reason Rhiannon can not be a mother to her child." He spoke with authority to the judge. The stern man wearing the robe in the center of the courtroom responded back hastily. "Her file states that she is schizophrenic, there is no cure for that. Do you realize this?" He answered the judge sure of himself. "Your honor, she is a highly functioning schizophrenic." My stomach churned as I saw the way the social worker gleamed when he looked at Rhiannon. Trevor, had a trial scheduled and was not present for this. It did not matter we were there on the behalf of Rhiannon, not us. As soon as we exited the double wooden doors, Polly, Sterling and I gathered on the bench. They noticed how upset I was. They said I should be rejoicing. I explained to them what my gut feeling sensed in the courtroom. "He is sleeping with her." They blew me off and said I was talking out of my head.

When we got in the car, Sterling scolded me. "Muffy, what is really wrong with you? Do you hate her so badly that you detest when someone says something good about her?" It was true, I honestly can not feel love for her. I know what I know. I knew that look. That was not a look of him making good on a promise. That was a sexual glare not a gleam. I let Jewel, know immediately. She also blew me off and said I have serious trust issues and perhaps I should talk to someone. I was not going to allow anyone to persuade my intuition. The nerve of Jewel, shocked me. Here she was not trusting an attorney. But putting her trust into a child protective service worker. I never breathed another word about my intuition. Holly Pearl, was indeed placed back into Rhiannon's custody. She would give us full visitation whenever we wanted or whenever we needed.

Her tiny steps chased Sterling around the apartment, much to his delight she followed him everywhere she went. She struggled with saying PawPaw, instead she called him Pup-Pup. He laughed about it and called his family to brag on this little diva. "All my life I have overcome obstacles went to college. Helped in the community, attempted to right every wrong. All to be a Puppy." He chuckled. "The greatest and only time I will answer as a dog." My heart delightful. Every place we took her we showed her off as if she was a princess. Rhiannon gradually abused her power over us. "Bring me cigarettes, pay my power bill, I am hungry." If Sterling refused these favors she would not allow us to keep Holly Pearl. I called that attorney myself after Sterling told me a variety of answers. None of which I was happy with. Trevor still has not returned one of my fifty calls.

Sterling did not seem furious when Trevor told him there was nothing he could do to help us. He said "Our state does not have grandparents rights and even if it did we would have no legal standing because I had fully adopted Rhiannon. Sterling is not biological family." I was livid. I wanted to go to his office and tear it up in effort to get my thousands back. Sterling ignored the tantrum I threw on him. "You would have blew through it on drugs anyway." Was his only defense. But at least I would have been the one blowing it. There was nothing I could do. It was just gone.

Jewel, said "Muffy, there has never been a time when I wished that I had been more wrong." She went on to blame Sterling. "I have never trusted Sterling. He has always been nice to me and on the outside he appears to be on the up and up. But there is just so much that we do not know about him. What's up with him being so secretive all of the time?" I am just glad he is still with me and providing me with stability. I do not want to know any secrets he keeps. I am not naïve. I know he has his flaws but I do not think it is anything serious. I am just content with his excellence in being the best Pup-Pup he can be.

Months would pass and bring us into the dry heat of the summer. We took our grand doll swimming every chance we got. I marveled at her bravery in the water and her great swimming skills. I knew she was skilled enough to go without the arm floats, but I left them on her to appease Sterling. He feared she would fall and get hurt. He really feared we would lose her in the water. Sun sparkling on the waves in the lake as we tossed her back and forth. Her cackle laughter was contagious. Other swimmers were delighted to see the fun that little girl was having. Nothing could have been better to my spirit than stopping for ice cream after leaving the lake. My energy was high and my mental illness was scaling low. I assumed the more I fought my demons the less powerful they would became. The more I focused on giving Holly Pearl the best life the more my life was going to become the best.

Yes, I still threw tantrum fits in public. Mostly, they were ignored with no consequences to suffer. Sterling and I celebrated eight years of being together. Stability. Nothing else mattered. For the first time in my life since I left my mothers house, I maintained the same residence. Sterling handled all of the bills, making sure they were paid on time. He grew tired of cleaning the messes that I made and adapted well to the disorder. We ate out against his wishes. I won that battle because he was tired of scrubbing pots and pans from food he could barely stomach to swallow. He got to the point where he begged me not to cook.

The days of relaxing in the sun and water were suddenly halted. Polly, called once more she was delivering bad news. Rhiannon and a neighbor had got into a dispute. Rhiannon sold her neighbor her foodstamp card. That should have been no big deal. Except for there was no balance on the card. The girl became furious when Rhiannon insulted her intelligence and refused to refund the girls money. That is when the tip reached child protective services about how one of their workers Fred, was making house calls to Rhiannon bringing her food and cigarettes. She even reported Fred, for bringing Rhiannon drugs. This had been the fifth report of this nature regarding Fred and a few more of his clients. This however had been the only one investigated. It would be our unlucky advantage this claim was reported to the only decent worker in the county. The one that did her job. The one that had faith even when she saw her co workers risk the lives of children to short cut their paperwork.

When they arrived they found Holly Pearl unattended and a very high Rhiannon walking up the street. She was instantly removed and placed back in Pollys custody. Due to the strict rules they imposed because I had been such a questionable person and Sterlings history of drug use. We could not even visit. Polly, needed us to help her out. But they did not care.

The worker wanted to genuinely help Rhiannon with getting the proper charges filed against Fred. She would not budge. He made it a habit of waiting on these women's psychiatric evaluations to come back, before he preyed upon them. All of his clients had perfect drug screens because he was not sending them for urine test. He swayed them with drugs and cigarettes and promised to help them get their children back. Not one woman admitted that they had been violated by that rotten belly freak. Each woman they interviewed believed Fred was their boyfriend. Because their cases had already been closed all Fred got was a discreet exit from his duties. Those women believed they owed Fred their lives and loyalty mattered. He even convinced a few including Rhiannon if she ever said anything negative about him demons would possess her. He convinced her he had magical powers. Only the clients with schizophrenia. I knew I hated him.

Polly cried and apologized. "I am so sorry, I should have listened to you Muffy." Jewel and Sterlings apologies flowed shortly thereafter. Nobody's apology mattered. Holly Pearl was gone and this time indefinitely. I did not want Holly Pearl to ever be returned to Rhi-Rhi. She risked our whole reason for being over one hundred dollars. An amount so minute that Sterling would have easily loaned her that amount. This time things would be different. The only thing that remained the same were the names on the documents and the

fact my twenty year old past was considered current. Polly was

deemed too old to handle a toddler and another child. Rhi-Rhi had

the nerve to turn against Polly making her fight with the

department unbeatable. She relished in the fight and turned her

mothering position over to her eldest daughter. We still could not,

visit just yet. The waiting for the courts to order Priscilla custody

seemed endless. Sabra opined that she was comforted for Holly

Pearl. She convinced me that Priscilla was young and vibrant. That is

what toddlers need. Priscilla had never done anything illegal or use

drugs. She was college educated. She could give Holly Pearl the life

she deserves to have. She said I should be on my best behavior and

let them see the changes in me and maybe they will let us visit on

holidays. Two years of social workers and court dates only to end

up childless.

CHAPTER EIGHTEEN

Time, went on. The people in my life did not. Alisha succumbed to a

diabetic coma. How unfair was that? How does God think that it is

okay to take the greatest people in my life? Sterling prays

everyday. He thanks God for our many undeserving blessings. He

ask for help and guidance. Why does God not listen to him? I held

Alishas hand for the last time. Her daughters were gracious enough

to invite me to the hospital to say goodbye to their mother and she

gasped for her last breath. I witnessed her suffering from the first

surgery when she lost her foot due to an infection. I listened quietly

when she told me how hard it was to put the cigarettes down and

even harder for her to lay the Pepsi down. Those two things she

attributed to what made her personality such a spitfire. I thought

she was going to jump out of bed and make a joke about the

hospital staff or even ask for a Pepsi. She did not. Her hands were

soft as a newborn baby. They were cold to the touch as if she was

already post mortem. I begged her to get up. I made promises that I will live right, never cuss in public, never again fuss at her for drinking too much Pepsi while I was guzzling a Dr.Pepper. I begged the nurse to do something to save her and felt like cussing her out when she just stood there. Her oldest daughter then asked Sterling to take me out of there. "She can not handled this so please take her home." That useless nurse could have done something I am sure. I do not understand why they make so much money to do nothing. If saving lives is their job why did I watch my best friend hold on for a few minutes more for life on earth. She did not want to leave her girls. She was a deserving of life as anyone else. Why did she have to die on us?

We no sooner pulled out from the red light when her daughter called and said she had passed. I screamed and cussed. I can not cope with grief, or devastation. My irrational behavior is part of how I process. My other friend and all of my family was really consoling to me. They knew she was the sister I wanted and never got. They knew I shared DNA with them. Alisha, and I shared a spirit. I can not fathom why she would leave this world knowing I can not bare a day without talking to her. I can not function properly without her humor and her warnings of the way I sometimes act out. Even, as an adult I do not understand death. It is so permanent, so forever. Unlike my various other messes which I always get through. Death, can not be fixed, or undone.

I do not remember the day of her funeral. It was all a blur. I was not high. I was disassociated with reality. I know her children were there and mutual friends of ours because of common sense. The last time I had attended a funeral she was with me. My only means of support. I am sure that I cried the loudest because I always do. Sterling, was there by my side. I can not recall his actions. It is just a blank day stored in my memory bank. I still see her from time to time. She comes to visit me when I am so sad I lose interest in getting out of the bed. I hear her words talking to me. We had dinner together the other night. Sterling and I was back at the Chinese buffet. She was sitting right beside of him. I was a tad bit jealousy of her glowing skin with no wrinkles. I heard her words and she kept up with the conversation with me just as clear as if she were still alive. Sterling looked shocked when I ordered her a Pepsi. He did not make a scene but I could tell it was frustrating to him.

I grow impatient waiting on her visits. I look forward to her pop ups. Sometimes when I am driving she hops in the car with me. Jewel tells me to fight it. She knows Alisha is not a ghost. She does not believe I am being haunted. She says it is all in my mind. I am unsure because she is so real and life like unlike the ghost you see on television or hear about in urban legends. I know she is real because she always fusses at me for my lack of concentrating while I am driving. She is solid on my erratic driving practices. We do not talk about her death or my life. Our conversations are about the people we see walking on sidewalks. We talk about their clothes and hair or the weather. I never get a chance to tell her how much I miss visiting her apartment or hanging out with her. She leaves just an unannounced as she arrives. Her short dark brown hair framing

her chubby face just as if she just got a haircut.

Jewel, explains to me that I am not normal. I do not listen to her.

There is nothing abnormal about having friends to visit with you.

Sterling, urges me to get help but I do not need to be medicated

and mummified. He wants me distracted. He does not want me to

know his slime behavior. He thinks I am oblivious to his

unfaithfulness. I know all of his dirty secrets. I do not confront him

because I have no intentions on leaving him. What is the use in

bringing it to light when I am not going to do anything about it? I

would be lost without him. Even Sabra told me to it is better to be

alone than disrespected, however with my condition I need

constant care. She claims I do not make rational decisions, and

putting him out would cause me more harm than good. She said I

have codependency issues. I wish that I did not. I wish I were strong

like her. She can cut a person off with no recourse what so ever.

Her spunk is diminishing. She is older now. She only leaves the house if Jewel takes her out. If she is not gone, she is asleep. Just laying in the bed letting each day be like the day before and the day after. She is at peace in her life right now, unless Scooter barges in drunk.

It is funny how life works out. He has been beaten and shot. Drowned and overdosed. Yet he is still alive full of life. My best friend and my son are in Heaven. I do not understand. I realize I have no right to refer to Champ as my son. Matter of fact it feels weird, like I am stealing a moment from Wava. I may not be able to show my feelings of love and adoration toward people properly but I still feel. Which is why I do not understand, death still.

Gloomy fall days, make my suffering worse. I am not the only person in the world with these issues. I am also not the only person in my apartment with severe issues. The infidelity has stewed in my spirit. The betrayal has marinated acerbating my mental illness. I have kept quiet so long it is now more out of habit than concern. I love that man. I have believed in him even when factual evidence showed me he was no better than me. I strived to make him proud of me when all of the while he was bamboozling me. He made me believe we had some kind bond that can not be broken. I could not take living his fictitious fairy tale one more second. He headed out of the door giving me his frequent lie about going to aid a sponsee. "No, not tonight. You are not. I think I deserve to know why you are unfaithful. Who is she or is it more than one." He shrugged and laughed it off. "You are not allowed to ignore me this time." I was calm up until he said "Muffy I am making a mental health appointment for you tomorrow." That is when I attacked him. I pelted his Yetti cup toward his face but missed by less of an inch. His pupils enlarged as if he had been smoking some kind of drug. He darted toward me and wrapped his hands around my throat. I went unconscious.

Sterling had been perfect as long as I agreed to live by his lying. The second I stood up for myself he counter attacked. When I came to consciousness, he was gone. I called and called his phone but did not get an answer. I covered my bruised neck and went out walking looking for him. Every street walking woman I passed made me cringe. I wondered if he had been with her. Even the friendly clerk at the gas station I suspected he had asked her for more than a lottery ticket and a full tank of gas. I wonder how many nights he rolled away from my touch because he had rolled into the arms of theirs. My tears eyes continued to fog my glasses as I walked aimlessly looking for him, looking for drugs, looking for nothing.

He returned at 10:20pm. Which is a normal time for him to come home. He did not speak one word to me nor did I utter a word to him. Our silence echoed off of the paneled walls for the next three days. We came and went. It was killing me inside. Every time he did not offer an apology felt like the wound being reopened. I did not mind the betrayal as much as I minded him blaming my mental illness. I did not mind him attacking me. I expected it. The fact that he used my mental defect to play on my emotions was the worst possible thing. I wished so badly Alisha would have came to visit me so I could have had someone to chat with. On the fourth day, the silence was interrupted with terror.

I opened the apartment door, to pitch black. Not one light on. I thought the power had been disconnected. I flipped the switch. A dim light casted over our tiny kitchen table. There Sterling sat with his face his his right hand. He was holding a .380 Rutger to his temple. I pounced like a scalding cat screaming "NOOOO, please DON'T!" he barely lifted his head my direction and pulled the trigger. Click. No, boom no nothing. He began to sob. I could not understand why he had hurt me so badly yet he is the one that felt like ending his life. I joined him in sobbing. He literally just had attempted to blow his brains out in front of me. Why? I needed him to help me understand. Why did we have to live with all of this hurt? My mind could not process fast enough to know that the click did not bring forth a boom. I saw the back of his head exploded a flaming glob of blood splashing against the refrigerator.

I was still screaming. Yet, he was alive and crying with me. The tears came down so hard and fast my head began to ache. His red wet face walked toward me. He knelt down beside of me and grabbed my hand. "I am so sorry for all the wrong I have ever done to you." Oh no he did not have to be sorry for anything because he was alive. That is all I wanted at that moment. Him to be real and in the flesh. I touched his face to make sure that I could feel him. To reassure myself he was not my imagination. Still alive. "I want to talk to you. I need for you to be quiet and after I am done speaking you can cut my throat if you want. You can leave me and never speak to me again and I will understand and accept whatever decision you make." It had been years since Sterling had talked to me about his feelings. I sat and waited on the words to come. "Muffy, I got fired today. After nineteen years. I was let go." I broke my promise and asked "Why?" His voice cracked. "Sexual harassment." "No, no they have no right to fire you. Who accused you of that?" I was ready to go beat, kick and stomp the woman who accused him. "Muffy, it is not one in particular. Eight women have came forward so far."

I shook my head no. I could not believe that my hero was telling me this. I could not believe that he wanted to kill himself over it. I hated those women who probably wore skimpy inviting clothes to work. They probably came on to him. "I will spit on them for lying on you. I want to know their names." "Muffy, I need you to listen to me. Things are going to get rough around here. Those women are not wrong, I was. I did everything they said I did and even more." I broke down crying once more. "Well..well what do you mean things are going to get rough? Did you rape them and you are going to jail. What do you mean?" "I am not a rapist. I offered the women extra hours on their paychecks if they would do things for me. I cooked the books to pay them sometimes even when they did not do favors for me." My stomach tilted as if I had been set on the rinse cycle in the washing machine. I threw up on the opposite side of where he was kneeling.

He went to get towels and Lysol to clean my mess. When he came back I said "What do you mean things are going to get rough? Are you going to jail for embezzlement?" No, I resigned to prevent being prosecuted. I let out a sigh of relief. I hated him at that second, but memories of how bad prison is bounced around in my head and I did not want him to be in a pod living off of ramen noodles no matter how much I hated him. I blamed myself. I should have put an end to his devilish behavior when I first suspected it. I should have been stronger. This would not have been happening if I would have been prettier, or not as crazy. "How will things get rough? You have plenty of money in savings. You have been penny pinching for years. You have always been frugal and money conscious. Plus you will draw unemployment." He fell into the fetal position. He cried out for God to help him. I never cried that hard over nobody's death. I never seen a man cry that hard. His wails were sincere and raised the hair on the nape of my neck. I went over to him and helped him sit back up. I hugged him and told him everything would work out ok. Then, the words he spoke hit me like a ton of bricks. "Muffy, you are not going to be able to forgive me for what I am about to say." How could what he have to say be worse than what he already had said.

"Remember, my friend Trevor?" "Of course I do that is the attorney that robbed us." He took a long deep breath and said. "No, no it was not him. Well at least not all him. We got high together with that money. I have been using every weekend since." I did not even know the man I was crying over, crying with. He stood up in meetings and proclaimed a sober life. He cussed me for days about being a drug addict. "I should blow your brains out now! But that is too good for you. You need to suffer. You judged me, you judged my family, you stopped speaking to Jewel because you blamed her for being with me while I was getting high. You told me I could not have the shoes I wanted because you were saving for us a house and this whole time you have been using."

"Muffy, I want to die over this. I feel so bad for living theses lies. How can I hold my head up and face the world tomorrow? Why should I?" I had no answers for him. I did not know. Random thoughts hit my mind, I could envision him messing with those women then coming home to me and I thought I wanted him dead or maybe just out of my face. In my family we do not give up. I may not be strong like those women who have struggled generations before me, but one thing is for certain. We do not give up. Truth was I did not want him to be dead. I really wanted all of this to be in my imagination. Life is so unfair. For the last nine years I lived to please him. To make him happy with me and the whole entire time he was making a fool out of me. "What else? What else have you done to disrespect this relationship? Disrespect me. What's next you are going to tell me you have tried to sleep with my friends.?" He let another tear fall. He looked me astonished, as if I had read his tarot cards accurately.

"Yes, I have done that too. I offered Piper money once. Fifty dollars. Years ago." I jumped up this time swinging hard blunt fist toward him. He put his arms up to block his face but I lit his chest and stomach up. "Go do it now, do it now blow your head off I hate you. I do not care." If I had not have walked in when I did maybe he would have reloaded the gun. Maybe he would have figured out why it jammed, and I would have walked in to his dead body. At that moment that I wished it had been the case. He let me hit him until I was tired and panting for breath. Where did we go from there I had no idea. My morals have often been compromised but I was not cool with living a lie. Throughout my life I have continued to live my truths no matter how unpleasant they may be. No matter how I looked in the community or to friends and family. I have kept it real. He passed the gun to me and begged me to kill him. I did not have the courage at that moment to take his life. As bad as I wanted him dead. I could not do it. I called Piper and cussed her like the dog she is. She should have told me. She should have came to me like a woman and said what he had asked her.

CHAPTER NINETEEN

Jewel, and Sabra had called it years ago but I was so infatuated. So stupidly in love I did not want to believe them. They had a better perspective of what was going on in my house than I did.

I stopped speaking to them at one point because I was tired of defending him to them. He knew it and let me disregard them as if they were crazy. That night his life did not end but life as we knew it ended. Nothing ever went back to being the same. He stepped back from speaking at meetings and rarely attended one. It was for the best since clearly they was not helping him. It was just something to do until he could go get high. A cover up to look good in front of his family. Some of those people at those meetings really are inspired by him. They believe the lies he lives and want to win over their addictions.

I missed talking to Piper but I still never called her. She was stored in my memories as if she was in the same place as Alisha. When I told Sabra everything, she said maybe the only reason she could think that Piper did not want to tell me was because she had taken him up on his offer. Piper swore that was not the case. Piper said she did not want to tell me because she did not want to hurt my feelings. What kind of nonsense is that. Jewel said she maybe right, because drug addicts do not think with good clear thoughts. Who knows, I will never know for sure. I only know what Sterling tells me.

We began a new phase in our relationship. One with total honesty and toxicity. We started getting high together. I only snorted cocaine. I never smoked anything. He only smoked it never snorted it. Eventually, he grew tired of smoking alone so we started going to Sabras to get high with Allison. She always knew where to get the best stuff. They lived smack dab in the center of town so getting supplied was never an issue. Sterling started hustling insurance so he was always getting a few grand. Due to the fact Allison knew

where to supply us and we never ran out of money Allison and I

never argued anymore over who did most of the drugs. We would

stay up for days then sleep for days at a time.

That was only possible in the apartment Sabra, had kept in such

great shape. Everyone had advised her to move years prior, but she

refused. She held on to that apartment as if it were a safety net.

She had always feared being homeless. She always tended to that

apartment as if it were her own house. For years, she had done her

own minor repairs. The complex had maintenance men for that but

she enjoyed using her electric screwdriver and Dewalt drill every

chance she got. She took pride in her home. We disrespected it. We

all knew if she was better we would have never gotten away with

drugs in her house. She was strict and concise. Any drugs that

entered through her door should be sold not done.

If Sabra would have had an ounce, of get up and care left in her there would have been no way we could have gotten away with our partying as long as we did. My choice of high mellows me out to a state of numbness. Chances are if she would have bounced down the stairs in a fit of frantic, I would not have been able to defend myself with words or physically. Sterling and Allison however, well their high caused paranoia so they constantly thought they heard her coming down the stairs. Good times were had by all.

People in our circle began to wonder where we disappeared to, but we vanished into each other. I suppose his deceit made it possible for me to be myself and him to be himself. He still paid the bills on time because he hustled. He would give boosters rides to stores so they could shoplift to pay for their habit. He charged them in merchandise not money. We did not pay for hygiene, cleaning products or groceries. He no longer pursued the interest of other women. We were always together. Sleeping, hustling or getting high. We became closer than we had ever been. So many nights I wanted him to be home with me and then he finally was. The man of my dreams I was able to live a nightmare with.

I still held a great amount of resentment toward Rhi-Rhi. She would never be allowed to stay another night in our house. Sterling still made sure when she called we ran to her aid. If she needed food, he would see to it she got food or cigarettes. It planted a seed in my mind that maybe he was especially fond of her. Not the way I had saw him toward her as a concerned step parent. Maybe he looked at her the way Fred did. Or the way he took advantage of those desperate single mothers who worked under him. That needed their jobs and would do anything to please their boss. I never shared those thoughts with anyone because it made me ashamed of myself for thinking they would be that low down.

She ended up pregnant again. This time she would not reveal the name of the father. That left me pondering that maybe my thoughts were pushing more toward facts. Sterling catered to her every need and I made sure that I abided by his wishes and did the same. We were on a much more comfortable level with each other so I asked him "Is that your baby? Is that why we have to cater to the sal that got Holly Pearl snatched from our life." He held no punches when he lit into me with cruel words. "Just because you can not manage to be a mother, you only worry about yourself does not mean we have to be horrible people. Just because you may be the cause of her mental illness do you not feel any remorse? Are you that evil? You can just not care. You know she loved that little girl and you know you are the reason she is mentally ill anyway. Maybe she inherited it from your crazy ass. Maybe she experienced some childhood trauma for having you as a mother. Neglecting and beating on her."

I hate to admit it but I was out driving alone and I saw her walking down the sidewalk with her belly sticking out, appearing to be panhandling, I would turn my face the opposite direction and keep driving. No matter the weather my reaction was the same. In my defense, there was nothing I could do for her anyway, especially with the way my circumstances were turning out. I gave her away to give her a good life. A descent chance in making it. All for her to end up turning out worst than I ever was. I wonder how many men are paying for her dignity. I wonder if those men even realize how dangerous she is. I pass her by and wonder when will the day be that I catch a news clip of her being arrested for murder. Or if she will be the one murdered.

I felt two inches tall. That was the lowest he had ever made me feel. He had talked about my mannerisms previously. That always made me feel less than worthy of love. Full of self doubt maybe he was right. I was so horrible that I thought the worst. I had to accept he was right her mental problems are what I had caused. So again, I tried to tolerate her. There was so much to accept to be with him. Accept that he had kept dark secrets for years. Almost a decade. Accept, that as much I loved him he did not give me any respect. Accept that, he made me feel less than him when the truth came out he was less than me. Less than zero.

His whole demeanor changed. He went from a gentle giant to a beast. He was only happy when he was getting high. Do not get me wrong I am happy getting high too. It is not the only time I can laugh or be happy. I started seeking our new friendships to replace Piper. That infuriated him. He told me to stop trying to befriend people I did not know. Implying that I was too crazy for people to love. It was embarrassing to him. When I came back on him with, " The reason, we are in this mess, is not because of my craziness. I have never been fired for begging for sex." He did not take well to my brutal honesty. He open hand smacked my face. His large palm covered my face. The sting numbed my whole face.

Sterling felt bad about his over reaction. The next morning I woke up to a new pair of Birkenstock's. He gave me the keys to his car and fifty dollar to spend it as I wished. I knew I had pushed him, too far. That was not the first nor would it be the last time he showed me he was in no mood for brutal honesty. It mostly came the day after we had stopped getting high. He felt immense guilt for giving

in to his desires of addiction. He tended to feel a great sense of

hopelessness. Sterling, had meditated, made amends to all that he

had wronged, he remained active in narcotics anonymous. He not

only did the twelve steps for years he lived them. He inspired others

that wanted to be clean and sober as he claimed he was. He

attended conventions held out of state with me in tow. We

celebrated recovery. He even submitted to God. Yet, and still when

the dragon knocked on his door he answered. He felt like he could

not make it leave.

When the drugs left his system. He became volatile. He took his

aggressions out on anything or anybody in his way and I was mostly

the one in his way. He carried that pistol as if it were his cell phone.

He feared being on the street without it. My attempt to confide in

Allison, about what life was like when he was not high was a fail.

She could not believe the same guy she parties with every weekend

from Friday to Sunday was the same person I spoke about on

Wednesday and Thursday. " He's a fun loving guy, you are just crazy as hell. You probably imagine it." Jewel knew when I spoke to her about it, these happenings were not a symptom of my schizophrenia. She lived with a narcissist. She was all to familiar with what I went through. She could not understand why I stayed with him. "Is your desire to stay high with him more than your desire to live?" She did not understand, that I still had more faith in him than he had in himself to get better. "What if he kills you by accident? You act oblivious to the news. You are acting as if you are invincible. What about ever getting to take Holly Pearl swimming again? Have y'all lost all hope in that day?" I suppose we had. She recited a lengthy list of consequences that she claimed was sure to come, if I continued living like the way I was. Nothing on her list matched the reality of what was coming.

I got to the point, I was scared to leave him. His mind took him to a darker place than mine ever could have thought about going to. He became distrustful, of me. He accused me of cheating on him.

Although I never did. I never even thought of dating another man during our relationship. Prior to our relationship from the moment I laid eyes on him. He was all I ever wanted. Those other men in my life were just passing time until he came around. He started to think that I would tell his secrets to his family. He told his sisters the reason he was fired was because the governor had cut funding to the program which funded his position. I went along with whatever lie he told them. After all they were being generous and compassionate their brother in his time of need. They paid our power bill in full every month. He did not feel like he owed them anything being as though they had kept up with their money and made remarkable financial decisions. It was unlikely they were going to miss the eighty dollars a month.

I would have never spoke a word to them about his business. Especially since the aftermath would have resulted in me having to cough up that eighty dollars. I too, was on unemployment again. Telemarketing jobs tend to be a fly by night career. One month they have so many contracts they have do to do a mass hiring. The

following month they can have no calls to make and the lay offs

begin. We were living a life that mimicked people lost in their early

twenties. Except for we were older. Our bodies ached more from

staying up for days. Our brains did not function well without

adequate. All of the signs directed us to restart recovery. We

ignored them and continued to be high, as if there were spirits

trapped in our souls we had no power to control.

Sterling, also accused me of shorting him on money. He had enough

to blow. He had enough to do whatever he wanted with. Where

was the harm in me spending ten bucks on McDonald's Big Mac's.

He made snide comments about how I should not eat fast food.

How it alters my appearance and makes not appealing to him

anymore. I took those cruel words to heart. The more he was

hurting himself on the inside the more hurt he directed to me. I

loved being high with him so much I did not act as if it bothered me.

I surely did not stop visiting drive thrus and guzzling a 12 pack of Dr

Pepper a day. I ignored his taunts and threats. All of those days and nights I listened to Heart back to back sing How Do I Get You Alone. Those ladies with their teased hair and mellow and raspy voices were singing to my situation. Funny how a song is a melody to your heart when you are feeling the words they vibe out. This is not what I thought I was signing up for. The reverence of my attraction to him was the difference between him and the other men I had encountered.

I learned the hard way, he was a masked monster. The reality was he was worse than anyone I had ever dated, or married. I am still able to ignore the voices in my head that dance around my thoughts whispering what a monster he really is. The more I allowed him to do to me, the more he did. The rougher he became. I started staying away from him as much as possible. I would wake up first and take the car, leaving him to rely on his feet for transportation. He lost all desire to do anything but sleep, get high and torture me. I escaped the torture part, by visiting family. I would go the pool and swim from the time the gates opened until they closed. He did not seem to mind my absence. It is possible, he was glad I was gone, because he was tired of mistreating me.

After he would lose his temper on me. He would always bring me gifts. Some how knowing exactly what I wanted or needed. I am not high maintenance. I have no need for jewelry. If I did I would probably lose it or misplace it. I am constantly losing my drivers license, bank cards or important paperwork. It is because I live in such a disarray of things. It is difficult to keep up with stuff. He would shower me with affection. His salty kisses on my swollen lips stung but I let him kiss me. I was afraid if I did not he would find someone else to kiss. Although, it was bad I was not ready to throw in the towel just yet.

CHAPTER TWENTY

Solemn faces gathered around once more. This time the sudden death would strike on Sabra's side of the family. The family that was always gathered laughing or cussing at holidays. Sometimes laughing about the cussing. Once more death grasped someone so deserving of a good life. My aunt Myra, had finally found a peace in her life. The issues she struggled with in her younger years seemed to disappear as she grew older. Her children had grown up. Her purpose was to help Jewel raise her girls. That was a job she adored. There is not as much stress in assisting with parenting than there is being a single parent.

Listen to me speaking as if she had the opportunity to grow old. Unfortunately that was not the case. This holiday season, was set to bring joy to their household but instead they got grief. She was Fifty seven years young. How unfair once more. Why are only the good dying young. I could not sleep for days when I heard the news. I hated to sound selfish but who was going to cook for us on holidays. Who was going to help Sabra cuss us out when our actions and attitudes needed checked. Who was going to laugh at my crazy?

Oh how my heart ached. It hurt for my family. Sabras mind, had already got as tired as her body. She did not understand her sister had passed. She thought Myra had went away for awhile. We kept explaining to her. She would comprehend but later in the the day, she would forget. This should have been my moment to step up. After all I am the oldest. I am the one who by rights should have it together. Again, I failed to be able to be that person someone could rely on. I laid looking at the ceiling thinking about how Jewels children must have felt. Myra, went hard for them. She was their rock.

Jewel, took it harder than I thought. She stood up in the center of the funeral home and spoke about her mother. Mainly warning us to make everyday with Sabra fabulous. Because we can plan for doctors appointments, but we can not plan for someone's heavenly appointment. I had never seen Jewel look so bad. My mind reflected back to when she was younger and had hangovers. When she was a rough neck young adult and spent more time fighting and doing foolish behavior. When she got out of prison. When she had surgery. Never had I seen her look so bad.

Jewel, is affectionately known as Diamond Lill. That is what Sabra, always joked and called her. Jewel, went to court dressed better than her attorneys. Not, this night. She wore a suit jacket that was too snug and a skirt that was too loose. If it had been anyone else in the world I would not have even noticed the hair out of place. It was oddly out of place on her. I never have seen her cry over anything. I never knew she was capable of such an emotion. It was not that long ago we were gathered around the table waiting on Myra to pull the turkey from the oven. Just like that with no warning. No chance to say goodbye. No chance to beg her to stay with us and not go. She was gone without notice.

As other family gathered in the house, Scooter, paced the yard. He wiped his tears with one hand and swigged from a brown paper bag with the other. "It should be me, not her." He told Sterling. Sterling responded back with "It is not our place to pick and chose the time we get to die." Scooter, had made that statement due to his scandalous lifestyle stretching three decades as a hilly billy rock star. Sterling, showed up for me in my time of need. So polite. He rushed me out of the house. We had an appointment to meet with Allison later in the evening. He needed to get back early enough to hustle up the money. He knew his family had learned decades ago not to loan him money in late evening hours.

Nothing was ever the same with any of them after that. Jewel, grieved she was too sad for me to bare my problems to. She tended to be a bit more agitated. Allison was not as happy as she was. I suppose she feared Sabra was going to be next. It was a harsh hit of

reality that tomorrow is not promised. Our lifestyles did not change

any. Scooter, remained a sot. Jewel, remained married to a demon.

I remained living in sin with the devil himself. If anything Allison,

treated her diabetes with more cocaine than insulin. Time marched

on but we did not march so fast. Sluggish, living our days waiting on

nothing just dissolving any potential, that we may have had.

Even with my mental illness, I know this should be the time of my

life when I am supposed to flourish. I am supposed to grasp onto

peace even if it is a tad bit. Just like Sabra, and Myra did. They had

come far, since their prime of being eighties ladies. A few years,

prior to that night, Sabra would have had her shoulder length

blonde hair pressed and fluffed up. She would have been wearing

something bright and amazing, sure to not have been seen in the

same shirt before. She grew into a stylish woman with grace mixed

with a hint of tactlessness. There she sat with a dazed look on her

face. Her clothes hanging from her shoulders like she had not

opinion as to what she was wearing to give her sister a final

goodbye. When I stopped my tears to look over at her, I knew it

would not be long before we going to be sitting in the same spot

giving her a final goodbye. Freedom to come and go as they

pleased. No worries about who they pleased. They had lived a

humble life full of tragedy and unfair to them in the timeframe for

triumph they were not here mentally or in physical to enjoy it. They

lived their lives unapologetic. There I was apologizing to the person

who caused me the most harm. I actually would tell Sterling I was

sorry I made him angry enough to beat on me.

Those days got old. I began to fight him back. I am stronger than I

look. I hit harder than I appear to be capable of. I can take a punch

as if I was trained to be a sparing partner in a boxing ring. Sabra

always told me "God, gives people strength to survive. If you lack

mental strength it will be compensated by immense physical

strength." I suppose she was right. When I finally returned the

punches he threw on me. He could not take it. He ran from the apartment stumbling as if he was dodging a hornets nest. When he returned I had him a solid white polo shirt laying on the bed. He loved dressing in golf shirts. His eye was a bit swollen but his glasses covered his bruising.

"Muffy, I am so sorry, for all that I put you through. I am sorry for any and every wrong I have done to you. Thank you, Thank you Thank you." "Wow, you must really love the shirt!" I replied. "It has nothing to do with the shirt, it is the fact that you have put up with me when I did not deserve it. You have took more from me and stood by my side when nobody else has been there. I know what I need to do." He knelt down and grabbed my hand. "Will you marry me, but not me today. Marry a better me? I am going to get help tomorrow. I took a long walk. I am so sorry so if you forgive me, and marry me I promise you I will get it together and be the husband, help mate you deserve."

"YES, of course. YES, a million times YES!" I exclaimed. That was the moment I had dreamed of when my first husband asked me to marry him. That was the moment I had been waiting for from way back when I was rambling through his things and breaking into his house. It was worth the wait. I did not focus another second on how badly he treated me. I looked for the day he was going to treat me good again. The next morning I waited with him in the emergency room. He tapped his feet to edge his nervousness. He was wise enough to know to get help he had to tell them he was suicidal during his evaluation. I missed him and he was not even gone yet. I knew they were going to medicate him and it would be worth the wait.

While he was gone, I had a junkie neighbor come in and help me clean. Miranda, was good company. She worked like a motel maid, separating our dirty clothes into baskets. She washed all of the filthy plates and pots and pans, from the weeks prior. She swept and mopped the cob webs from the corners of the floors. Miranda, was pregnant but that did not deter her meth addiction. She had

sores on her skin that looked like gun shot wounds. I paid her a

twenty dollar bill as she lifted the last bag of trash out. Miranda,

had once been a tiny little beauty queen. I did not care enough to

hear her back story. They are all pretty much the same stories

coming out of different mouths. Pretty girl, good home, bad home

normally made no difference. Pretty girl meets bad boy, gets strung

out ends up in this building.

A week before Sterling was going to be released from the hospital, I

got lonely. I hate being by myself. The voices get too loud. When I

saw Rhi-Rhi walking in the rain, I invited inside the car. I drove her

to Wendys. We ate so much. Her stomach was so large she used it

for a tray to eat on. My mini-me, followed suit when I tossed my

trash in the floor. That made me laugh. The more I tried to avoid

her, the more I seen there was no need. We were one. We shared

something horrible. I would later learn we had a lot more in

common. "Can I stay with you for a little while just until I can get my check?" Before giving the request much thought. I said "Yes." No doubt she was about to pop. The first night she slept and snored so loudly I had to wake her up to roll her over. The next morning I took Rhi-Rhi to the store and she stole a whole shopping cart full of junk food. Again, a trait she got from me I would rather eat snacks than meals. After we got back and tore into the potato chips Miranda came knocking. "Is there something else I can do for you for some money. My boyfriend left me with no cigarettes?" Rhi-Rhi, jumped up and introduced herself as my daughter. She passed Miranda two cigarettes. Before the day was up we all three were sitting at the table playing Yahtzee. I could not stand the smell of the smoke so I made them walk down the stairs and go outside. They both chain smoked. They compared pregnancy and homeless stories. I just listened.

I was not comfortable sharing my time of youth and stupidly pregnant. It was not such a joyous time for me. I kept my thoughts to myself and let them blab while I won game after game. I was having a good time with them. We were all three drug addicts but having a blast not on drugs. We drank soda after soda. By the time Miranda was ready to go I had bought her two packs of cigarettes for cleaning all of our mess up. Thank God I never picked up that disgusting habit. It was like a slumber party. Just like back in the day when I would stay with Myra. We were down to two when Nate knocked on my door looking for his woman, Miranda.

Nate, was gargantuan. Surely, he played football, hockey? Both? Something? He was the type of drug dealer who hustled and risked his freedoms for the glory of being able to restock his supply. He made little money. He wore nice shoes but that was because of Mirandas monthly disability check. Miranda, was tiny despite being pregnant. I could not imagine that tiny little girl having to fight that ginormous man. Nate wore, a fitted hat. A real fashion model for this neighborhood. Two hundred dollar shoes for walking. He stayed gone more than he stayed at home. The rare occasions that he is home you can be assured Miranda will be seen running for her life, or heard yelling to help save her life. Nate, has always been pleasant to me in passing. I have never had any other dealings with him.

CHAPTER TWENTY ONE

In the spring time an unusual cold front hit these mountains. Sterling still tucked away in the hospital with a week to go. This particular Thursday night brought more than I could bare. I ran to the grocery store. I had only been gone thirty minutes. When I came back all of Merrill Street was blocked off with emergency personal. I was close enough to see the gurney going inside of my building. I threw the car in park. I jumped out without even shutting the door. Times of chaos tend to make me panic. I made my way through the crowd. I heard a junkie say to me. "That's your apartment they are going inside of." I pushed through some more people wedging my way through to the main entrance. "Step back ma'am we are bringing them out.." I screamed at him. "Who are they?" He sternly ordered me to "Calm down." Then an officer intervened. "Ma'am do you live here?" I told him that I did. "Ma'am is that your daughter staying with you?" "Yes, please just tell me what is happening." I pleaded.

"Your daughter just gave birth in the bathtub, congratulations it's a boy." He stepped away to allow room for them to pass by. I ran upstairs and my bathroom was a horrible mess. Blood was everywhere. I threw up in the wastebasket and walked out. I locked the door and dashed back down the steps jumping in the car. I went to the hospital. I was excited. I was thrilled, yet in shock. We I got to the labor and delivery room I knew exactly what baby was ours even though I could not see the name tag or the plastic bassinet. I went to Rhiannon's room, and waited for what seemed like forever for them to bring the boy into us. Fact was due to state laws she had already lost her parental rights to two other children. Child protective services would not allow her to leave with this one. The nurse brought the baby in. Oh how I adored him. I inhaled that new baby scent. The nurse asked her all kinds of questions. I barely paid any attention to what she was being asked or how she answered. I was too busy loving on that heavenly ham of a child.

His face did not resemble ours yet, still looked very familiar. It is hard to tell when they are so new and wrinkly like pugs. When the nurse asked, about the father. I felt the stare from Rhiannon cut through soul. "Sterling is his first name and I am not sure about his last name" she said. They nurse went through of a series of other questions. "Do you have a history of mental illness? Do you have any other children?" And so forth. I placed the bundle of joy back in his bassinet. I walked over to Rhiannon. My temper was swelling up inside of me like water bubbling over a pot. I had intended on jerking her hair out by the root and punching her in the face until I broke every bone that held her sorry mouth together.

When I approached the bed as the nurse was stepping away. She was open for me to injure at that point. I saw something in her eyes. I seriously saw how sick she was. How this had not be the first time a man who was supposed to help her in life hurt her even more. I saw how I had been treated in my lifetime. "Muffy, I am really sorry. I never wanted to do it. He made me. He told me that if I did not he would tell you bad things about me and you would hurt me or never speak to me again. All of those times I saw you pass me by I thought he had already told you. He bought me cigarettes when I would do things with him. Muffy, I really really told him no, but he kept saying things like if I did not please him it would mean I was bad and those voices in my head will get worse. I am scared when I hear them. And I didn't want it to get worse, you know he is a warlock and talks to the devil about us."

That outrageous story probably would not have went over well on anyone else. I understood how scary those voices are. I knew exactly how bad witches put fear into her heart. There had been times during Halloween seasons that she would have full panic attacks inside of a store, that had decorated with witches. I remembered him reading a book about witches and warlocks prior to her staying with us before. I knew that she was telling the truth. I could not hold my composure together. I fell on top of her sobbing and hugging her. "I am so sorry, this happened to you. I am sorry I did not take better care of you, in your life." Rhiannon was too sick to understand that she had indeed been raped by Fred and now Sterling.

I had to pay someone to bring Allison to the hospital to get me. There was no way I could drive. That is when I lost all love and respect for Sterling. He basically raped her got her pregnant and lost his mind behind it and ran off to be medicated to cope with this. Allison, said "Muffy, you got to pull it together. I love Rhiannon but who knows who that baby's father really is. You know these streets eat her alive out here. So lets get a DNA test done and just go from there." That would have made sense except for the baby has a birthmark on his stomach in the same shape and spot Sterling does. They also have the same nose and chin. Allison made the joke "All fat bald white dudes look alike." We laughed even though it was not funny.

Our healthy baby was not in fact healthy at all. In the early morning hours he started seizing. It was obvious the baby was going into severe withdrawals from the opiates and meth she took while pregnant. Just like our personalities split that is the way my feelings for her split. I felt pity for her. I was apologizing for all wrong I had ever done to her. Someway I felt responsible for what he had done to her. I relied on him. That showed her she could trust and rely on him as well. It put her into a position to be harmed by him. When I first suspected it I allowed him to convince me my craziness was putting unrealistic thoughts in my head. That baby did not deserve to be born a junkie. I hated her for that. I could not stand the sight of her. When social services from the hospital called to tell me the baby would be placed in foster care. I hung the phone up on them. I was not going to fight that horrible agency again. I did not want to be bothered with her or any problems. I called a Christian friend of mine and asked her to put that baby boy on their pray list. I was done once and for all.

Sterling was released from the hospital just when we expected. I did not greet him with open arms. I picked him up from the hospitals parking lot. We drove to fill his prescriptions. He complained about my driving. I looked at him. "You should worry about your son and the mess in the bathroom I have left for you to clean." "Muffy, are you having another psychotic episode? you know I do not have any children?" I screamed so loudly cussing him that I could not even understand my words. We walked into a clean but rancid smelling apartment. I did not say much to him. I tried to provoke him into hitting me so I could get us both out of our misery. He resisted the invitation. He gagged while scrubbing the week old disgust in bathroom. He complimented me on keeping the apartment so clean. It was obvious he was not going to admit to what he had done.

If I put him out I would have no car. I would have no money to pay the power bill. I would have no money to party with. I had nowhere else to go. I just bottled up the hurt. He took his medicine and fell asleep. I watched his lips flutter and prayed he would not ever open his eyes again. That would simplify everything. What kind of man would take advantage of someone as sick a Rhiannon? I assumed the same type of man who had taken advantage of me for the past ten years. As he continue to melt into his slumber I remembered the rage he felt against Fred, the freaky social worker. "How horribly disgusting of a human is he?" Those were only his exact words. Freds actions emboldened him to do the exact same thing. For years, Sterling, has spoke against me being a horrible mother. Now, he had a child he has no interest in seeing or caring for.

He works so hard at worrying about what society thinks of him. I wonder what his family and sponsees would think if they knew about this. It is no wonder he wanted to sleep his problems away. I lost the ability to focus on anything else. He knew when he was paying her she was going to buy drugs. He knew she was pregnant. He knew that baby may have been his. The monster dwelling inside of him did not care. I had nobody to talk to about this except Jewel, and Allison. Jewel, offered condolences but could not offer any advice as to what to do. "Muffy, this is the unimaginable. I do not know what to tell you. I have never experienced nothing even close to this." Jewel was infamous on sharing the lessons she had learned in life with those around her, in hopes they would not make the same mistakes. And if she had the solution she would freely share to keep us from trying to figure it out on own our and making bigger messes.

Allison, also had no words of wisdom for me to follow by. All she could offer was moments for me to escape my reality. I took every invite to party with her that I could. Sterling, his recovery lasted

from Tuesday morning to Friday evening. We were right back

staying up the entire weekend again. I wanted to die anyway at that

point. I just was not courageous enough to jump off of a bridge or

slit my own wrist. Even though Sterling and me resumed our

relationship. I was not happy. I had never felt so all alone in my life.

Alisha visited me more frequently the sadder my days became. It

was never the same. I needed her to cook for me. I needed to sit

with her on the patio and sip soda and have long in depth talks. She

was so book smart. She could have been anything she wanted to be

in life. Instead sex made her a mother before love made her a wife.

She was a great mom, who raised great women. To me, that is just

an important of an accomplishment as any. Her riding shot gun to

the store with me never has replaced the things I miss the most

about her. I can not stop grieving her death.

CHAPTER TWENTY TWO

While cities and towns decorated lamp post with flower basket and placed mini flags on road sides and families gathered around for grilling and BBQing in celebration of Memorial Day. Sterling, Allison and I partied as usual. Sterlings wallet was loaded with thirty one hundred dollar bills. He had cashed another insurance check and we headed to Allisons to escape. He never made mention of the baby neither did I. We were just letting life live us. Each day he became harder and harder to figure out. He was the same man who nursed me after my surgery years prior. He was so loving and caring to me. He was also the same man who had choked me when I brought his deceitfulness to light. The same man who cared for Holly Pearl, better than her own mother could. He was also the same man that took advantage of her mother as well.

As always Friday vanished into Saturday. Saturday night blended into Sunday morning. Even though he still had money. There were no drugs to be found nowhere. The party had came to a halt. He

drove us home, while I dialed every number of anyone I could think

of in an attempt to get more. This was always the worst part of the

high. Running out. Nothing could be found nowhere. I even asked

Nate, if he could help us. His sober eyes gave me the answer before

his voice did. "Man, there is nothing nowhere." Sterling, did not

want to hear that answer neither did I. There was nothing we could

do but accept the party was over. We got into the apartment which

was now the pig stye, we had grown accustomed to living in.

Sterling started cussing me over the filthiness. I let him vent his

anger because he was somewhat right, and I was too tired to fuss

back.

Thirty minutes later he still had not let up. His vicious words got

harsher and harsher. I knew it was time to put him in his place.

"Maybe, you would have time to clean, if you were not so busy,

raping the mentally ill. How about you go find your dope feign son

and raise him since you want to be a daddy, and dictate orders?"

Sterling became in raged. I saw the red glowing evilness of the devil, in his face when he charged at me. I fought him back but my punches were not landing. He lifted me off of my feet with a punch to my face. While I lay crying on the floor his giant feet hopped on my chest. I curled up to prevent any more kicks. Something made that monster stumble. He fell back and became unsteady on his gait. Which gave me the opportunity to jump up to get away from his stomps. I had no time to figure out if what was happening was real or just in my mind. He had hit me before but never with so much force and trauma. I pivoted to the kitchen. He charged toward me once more.

"Go Away, Stop. Don't take another step!" I demanded. I grabbed the dull butcher knife from the drawer. I pointed toward him and dared him to take another step. When he came within my arms reach I stuck him in the chest. He let out a blood curdling scream. I stuck him again this time in the throat. His throat began to make a rattling sound. I looked him in his eyes. He was not one bit sorry for anything he had ever done. His irises were red. I saw horns

protruding through his forehead. I was in a panic. I knew I had to

end this monster once and for all. The knife grinding against his

neck bone and made a sawing sound as I pulled in out. Blood was

squirting everywhere. As if someone had turned on a water hose. I

stabbed him again this time in the stomach. The dull knife struggled

breaking through his obese belly. I pushed in further in with all of

my might. I could hear the squishing sound as I twisted the knife

deeper and deeper.

I am unsure how many times I forced the knife into his body. I

stopped counting after six. Finally, he was laying lifeless in a lake of

blood. I thought the was befitting considering his soul was probably

in a lake of fire. I fidgeted and paced as to what should I do next. If I

called the police I knew I would be in prison for the rest of my days.

Who was going to to believe and ex con over his prominent family

name? As much love as he earned in the community nobody would

ever believe I've been living with a monster. I knew better than to call anyone for advice. I pulled a blanket off of the bed to sop the blood up with. For the first time in my life. I cleaned my own living space. I used magic erasers and bleach to scrub the blood splatter from the wall. I am positive I missed some around the baseboards. I kind of enjoyed the clean scent of the bleach. His blood flowed from the knife down the sink drain. I washed the knife so much my feet began to swell from standing in one spot for so long.

The large blanket was saturated in blood. It had not absorbed the way I had intended. I lifted the heavy blood soaked blanket and toss it in to a black hefty bag. That blanket must have weighed fifty wet pounds. I was tired at that point. My adrenaline kept me going. My mind was racing yet I was able to focus toward completing the task of getting the mess up. For someone who had spent their entire life evading the task of cleaning I surely had stepped up. The blood smell had started to sour. It had been two hours passing since the first knife wound. The smell was making me nauseated but I fought to keep it down. I grabbed another blanket and sloshed it through the blood clots and spills. Large swirls of red surrounded the living room floor. His creepy eyes were still opened. I sensed his big blue eyes watching me.. I bent down and closed his eyes and placed his glasses back on his face as if I had attended mortician school.

Once the red swirls had faded into the wooden floors. I had to move him. I dreaded that. He was not a small man. Dead weight. Literally. I found that strength Sabra always insisted that I had. I suppose with the amount of blood he lost it made his body lighter. Yet, it still felt like I was dragging a refrigerator through the apartment. Thank goodness for my tiny nest. I did not have to drag his body far. I was exhausted but I kept lugging and pulling as I huffed and puffed. Sweat roll from my head and neck. I pushed him beside of the bed. I took bleached soaked towels and cleaned his neck. The way that knife grinded, I was surprised he still had a neck. In the center of his throat was just a deep wound the width of the butcher knife. He would not fit underneath until I raised his arms above his head as if he were swinging from monkey bars. He had already got cold to the touch by the time I stuffed him between the bed rails and floor.

My sweaty blood stained, wet clothes starting sticking to my skin. I was disgusted how his blood dripped on my face as I lifted my shirt off. I showered and used every bit of soap. When the water warmed back up I showered again and again. The drain sucked the blood down just like on a Psycho movie. I tossed my clothes in to the hefty bag with all of the blankets and towels. Then I showered again.

At a quarter to three, I was tired of cleaning and lifting and worrying. I left the monster under my bed. I went to Allison, I had eight one hundred dollar bills. I knew with that kind of money she could find me something to escape with. She noticed me being antsy, and my anxiety being over the top even for me. She interrogated me. I would not say nothing. I was not even sure if it was even real, until she pointed out my bruises. "Muffy, you look like you been in a car wreck. Did you wreck Sterlings car?" I shook

my head no and replied "He beat me." Abruptly, her head spun

around. "Whoa, whoa, I was thinking when you said he hit on you,

you was meaning smacked you to calm you down. I did not know he

was fighting to hurt you. He was always so loving to you." Then she

giggled in her snide way and said "So what did you do? Kill him?" I

never answered I just ignored her and dumped the scrabble tiles

out.

We got high and played scrabble. We got higher and played more

scrabble. Finally, I did not even want any more drugs and neither

did she. I asked if she had some peroxide so I could put it on my

wounds to help heal my injuries faster. She obliged. I remembered

from years ago when Scooter got shot they cleaned the blood up

with peroxide and bleach. I knew I should do the same. I got home

to a dimly lit second floor dungeon of death. I spent hours more

mopping blood up with bleach and peroxide. Surprisingly, enough

after I took the hefty bags out there were no signs of anything wrong, other than my place was much cleaner than normal. I slept

in the recliner that night and many nights to follow. I left all of his

belongings just where he had left them. Other than his cell phone. I

used it daily to send texts to people he normally stayed in contact

with. I pretended he was back in the hospital. Everyday, I would

soak a bleach rag and lay it near his body. When I would miss him I

would try to lay in the bed. I had to put vapor rub under my nose to

mask the smell.

Miranda, came over to visit. We shared some laughter and she

vented her life's frustrations with me. Soon, Nate would come and

chat with us then they would leave. I discovered I liked Nate, more

than I should have considering I knew the type of person he was to

Miranda. A week or so passed and then I was buying drugs from

him or he was having me go give him rides to restock his supply. I

did not condone his behavior but he shared his drugs with me and I

started loaning him the car when I did not feel like driving them

where they wanted to go. Nate, would divulge secrets to me about his business. For some reason he trusted me. He made a reference comparing us to Snoop Dog and Martha Stewart because of our obvious differences.

On a Monday morning, I was inside of the police station. My crying was not theatrical. It was real. I reported Sterling missing. They turned me away because I was not a relative. They were adamant that it had to be a relative to file the report. I called Sally, and explained to her that Sterling left the Sunday before and had not been home since. I told her how he leaned down and kissed me bye and said "I am going for a walk." He has not answered his phone or anything. I took the phone on Sunday and threw it between a bank and a convenient store. I figured some drugged out junkie would find the phone and that would be that. Sally, went to the police station and filed the report. She told the officer that Sterling had suffered from suicidal idealizations for years. The officer told us not to panic. He was probably out of state in a rehab and Hippa laws prevent them from investigating places like that. It honestly never occurred to me that they may come to my apartment searching for clues in finding his whereabouts. They did not. Not one knock on the door. I was getting creeped out that they would knock and find his body.

A week later his face was plastered on the news and social media. So many people reached out to assist with a search party. I let them organize as many as they had time for. I just declined the invitations to be a part of it. I told the concerned friends and citizens "It means the world to me that you guys are willing to sacrifice your time, to help me. I am in no shape for that. And if I were to find him it would kill me." The monster was still under my bed. Yes, I grieved for him. I could hear him walking through the apartment at night. I even woke up once to him watching me sleep from the door way. The detectives were all so kind to me. They spoke to me about every tip they received. Even the crime stoppers tip that actually accused me of killing him.

I was being questioned. The extremely handsome detectives,

implied that my first husband came up missing as well. I told them I

had left that crazy man and had not heard a word from him since

the day I left. I was not actually lying. It was true I left, true I had

not heard from him. These detectives were not your coffee and

donut stereotypes Hollywood depicts. The tall caramel complected

one, with full round lips and long eyelashes looked like he had made

a fortune as a model prior to becoming a detective. His sweet

looking partner with high cheekbones that bragged about his Indian

ancestry showed no reaction or reason to believe they were talking

to the person who ended Sterlings life.   I told them about my

mental illnesses and offered them to run a background check on

me. Which they had already done so. They found my crime was

nonviolent and I was no threat to anyone. They went on to quiz me

on the mental state of Sterling. I explained to them that day I came

home and found him at the table with the gun to his head. I told

them about the other instance when he had called me crying and

saying goodbye, and telling me if he could get his nerve up I would never see him again. That day Allison and I happened to be together riding around when I got that call. She heard what he had said to me.

She snatched the phone asking him where was he? Surprisingly enough he told her. We pulled up to the edge of a cliff. She leaned over and saw him walking along side of the railroad tracks. She could see the pistol to his temple as he walked. She climbed down the man made path built by hikers. Green moss covered the rocks. Stray ivies entangled throughout the path. I kept my feet planted as if I were going to grow roots. I was too clumsy to be climbing. If I would have made it down there and the gun would have went off I could not handle that. Allison, on her butt and knees made her way to him. I do not know what words had exchanged by I saw him hand her the pistol. He assisted her back up the path. As we all got back in the car. She looked at him and "Yo, man you a little too damn crazy. Why do you want to go through all of this. Live your life!" Here eyes rolled and lips curved up she let out a smh and continued

"Here I have been struggling to live and survive my whole life and there you are trying to take yours. We ain't ready for you to go meet Jesus just yet." Sterling agreed "Yeah, I get like this sometimes, I know it is crazy."

The detectives asked me to describe that exact location. Which I did. Three days later they had cadaver dogs searching the area. They promised me that if his body was out there due to the temperatures and the wind blowing they would have found him. People from the Fellowship home continued there search parties. By this point, they had figured he had jumped from a bridge and it was possible he may had hitchhiked to another state. The tips stopped coming in. The search party volunteers had dropped from thirty down to two. The monster was still under my bed and the bleach had stopped masking the smell of his decaying body. It had been horrible in my bedroom a few days after he passed. The smell of rotting flesh, is the worst scent I have ever inhaled. It gets under your nostrils. So, even when I was not in the bedroom with him, or in the apartment, I still could smell the poisonous scent of his murdered decaying body.

CHAPTER TWENTY THREE

Fortunately, I was such a nasty housekeeper and my buildings stairwell reeked from other bodies that took their final heroin doses. Those bodies were usually picked up fairly quickly. The smell of death always loomed. It was getting to the point the whole house was reeking like rotting cabbage and eggs. I had only slept in the bed a few nights because I could not take the smell. I had no other option but to move him. I had to have help to do it. I had to lift the whole entire mattress and box springs off of the bed to drag him out. He was so bloated I pulled and pulled but he would not budge. I had to get help. I just could not trust anyone with my secret. With no other choice I decided to shoot my shot with Nate. I waited on him to stop by. He knocked on the door. As soon as I opened it he gagged. "Muffy, oh do not cook whatever that is you cooked no more, that shit is awful. Girl, you better get you the whole shelf of air freshener." He said to me. "Come in here for a minute." He put his shirt over his nose and mouth and came inside. "Look, I got some money. Well I got access to some money. Four hundred dollars if you will help me." His eyebrows raised. "Man, I ain't killing nobody for you not for that kind of money, anyway! What do you got in here anyway? A damn dead body?" I looked up at him and said "NO, I do not want you to kill nobody. I have already done that. I need you to get rid of him. You can not use my car. You can not tell a soul." I could not risk letting him know that I actually had the cash on me. I did not want him to rob me then report me. I knew I had built up enough trust with him he knew my word was my bond. I explained to him the exact location Sterlings body needed to be hanging.

Two hours later, Nate came back. When I opened the door he almost blinded me spraying Glade air freshener. I looked up at him he had hospital gloves on and a surgical mask. His mother was a NICU nurse. He borrowed her car to ransack her console. I helped him lug Sterling to the living room door. "I got this, go get the money. And if when I come back and you ain't got my money I promise you you going in with him." Ten minutes later I met him in the dark wooded area. He used a black wheel barrel meant for industrial use to haul his body two miles down the railroad tracks. We went up an embankment. I held the flashlight while he tied a rope around Sterlings neck. Then we hoisted his rotting body to a tree branch.

He looked ghostly swaying like a pendulum in the moon light. I still have not chased that vision from my mind. We walked back to our cars together and I handed Nate, four one hundred dollar bills. It was still not over. It will never be over. Sterling still visits me like Alisha does. Sometimes he wakes me from my sleep screaming and begging me to help get him down. I shake it off. I know that is only his haunting of my mind. I did not want to end his life that day. At least he no longer suffers with what people think of him. He no longer has to be a people pleaser or fight the dragon on his back. He is at peace and that is something I will never have.

I used alcohol, bleach and peroxide daily to rid the smell of feces Sterlings body left lingering. Miranda helped mop in pine sol and bleach. I was not too worried about her telling anyone anything. After all rumor had it she had actually called to dispute Sterlings missing date. She had got so high, she thought it was August instead of June. Nobody took her serious. I had not spoke one word of Nate and my secret and he vowed to me he had not told her. He did not want her to know he had any money. A few weeks passed and my apartment was back to smelling like moldy laundry and week old household trash.

Nate, spent his money on shoes and drugs. If I did not comply with his favors of loans or whatever he needed from me. He would say "Luminal." He watched so many forensics files shows he probably could have solved the crime before he even knew I had done it. And most likely would have if an reward would have been offered. He was able to extort possession of my car more than I had it. When Allison would call wanting me to take her somewhere I had to say I could not because Nate had the car. "What does he have on you? What does he know about you that you do not want nobody to find out?" She would make accusations like that. I would blow her off. I was always amazed at how much she always knew without knowing.

One afternoon Nate, was supposed to come take my car as if he owned it. He did not show up which was odd. Nate, had got so bold over using my car, which he never put a drop of gas in, he would cuss me out for my fast food trash in it. I suppose weeks of mail and sales papers and useless coupons added with month old French fries and half eaten burgers had to be a nuisance if you were not used to it. I had drove like that for years, I was used to it. Hours later, after I came back home from random wandering in the car. Hours later after I returned from random wandering while driving a loud pounding knock was banging on my door. My heart sunk to my knees I knew it had to be the police. Either they had found Sterling or they were coming to arrest who had killed him.

I opened the door, to a pale distraught Miranda. "He's gone, he's gone this time forever." Without having to ask who she was referring to I knew she was meaning Nate. "Where did he go?" I asked with sincere concern. "They found him." She broke down into sobs I could not understand her words. "They found who?" I shouted. I just knew she implying Nate was in jail because they had found Sterling and I was next. My heart began to pound out of my chest. She collapsed in my arms. "They found Nate, dead this morning." Nate, had been found dead due to speedballing. He snorted so much cocaine he could not go to sleep so he ate a handful of Valium and went for a walk. He was found leaned over on a green metal bench not far from our building.

God, keeps me alive for a reason. A reason I do not know. I am sure he has a plan for my life. As scared as I was to be alone. I packed my favorite shirts and shoes in Sterlings duffel bag. I jumped in my car and drove. I headed toward I-77 with no particular destination in mind. I looked over to the passenger seat. Alisha, said "Go south, go far south. Try Louisiana, " I questioned her "Why Louisiana?" She said "Why not?" I passed through Georgia fighting the urge not to stop in Atlanta. A place I have always wanted to go. I sped on through Alabama resting in Montgomery. I was closer to white sands than I ever have been in life and yet I continued on abiding my Alisha's instructions, taking the exit toward Mobile. A thousand interstate miles later I was driving on crowded narrow streets. I was panicked. I am not a good driver. Turtle paced bumper to bumper traffic stressed me. I beat my frustrations out on the steering wheel. A few rights and a couple of lefts the road widened. I could get through with ease. I no longer wanted to. I wanted to mesmerize my mind with the tall buildings. The smells of mufalettas, and beignets filled the air. Homeless people were being stepped over by tourist. Every doorway and every alley appeared to be a resting spot for the homeless. I thought that to be cruel, but for some reason I thought this is where I was always supposed to be. This diverse streets seemed to be accepting of me. No, matter how good the food always smells on these streets. The humidity is a lot to bare. It feels like you are in a sauna even in the mid morning hours. There is always the faint smell of marijuana in the distance. It does not have to be Mardi Gras, for the block to celebrate. A celebration of life is constant here. This is my tribe, not the scared to leave the town where they were comfortable doing what they were always used to doing. The ghost that haunted these streets were just as visible as the ghost that haunt my mind. It is my normal here.

Four months after I found my new home I heard that a couple of hikers found Sterlings body swaying, exactly where Nate and I placed his badly decaying body. By the time the weather and insects took their turn eating what remained of him, they had to use dental records to identify him. Sally, had him cremated, to my knowledge his ashes are still in a card board box, with other forgotten family members that relatives want to forget.

This had not been the first time I left the steepness of the mountains to embark on a journey with southern sunshine. When the news was casting stories about the Clinton inauguration and snow was spitting in the north. I was basking in the perils of the South Carolina shoreline. I loved the winters there. The ocean was so peaceful in the off season when no tourist hoarded through the sand. The nightclubs that had lines stretching for three hundred yards in July, mimicked the smaller dive bars I was accustomed to. Being near the waves made me want to drink less. I saved more money that way. I was able to go to the bar more. I ended up in a brief but bad relationship. I became homesick and took the first

thing in motion back to the mountains.

After Sabras sudden heart attack, Allison moved away too. Nobody

thus far has made it to see their seventieth birthday. Maybe, the

nutritionist and dietitians know the facts they preach about if it

taste good, it can not be good for you. Coca-colas in Myras case and

desserts in Sabras case may have been the reason they had to leave

this world without the chance of growing real old.. I miss them so

much. I even miss Sterling, but not as much. He stays with me and I

feel his presence. I do not feel guilty of murder. He was suicidal

anyway. He was smart enough to know me after ten years. He had

to know my kindness to him was real. My anger is dangerous. He

took the chance, sometimes I can not help but to wonder if maybe,

he wanted me to kill him. After all he had multiple failed attempts

at suicide. Perhaps, he lacked the nerve to do it himself and decided

to keep pushing me until I snapped. I do not feel like a murderer. If that is even a thing. I block it out of my mind just as if it was any other misery I have caused or, misery life has caused me.

The last I heard, Scooter was living out his hillbilly rockstar fantasies in the swamps of Georgia. Although I will never visit, because he would not dream of extending the invitation. He has never forgave me for how I treated Rhiannon when she was little. If he did invite me, there is little chance I would put forth the effort to go. If he needed me to save his life, I would go but only if it were a dire need. Without ever having been to see him, I vision him belligerently drunk, standing over a grill cooking the best meat. Then being too drunk to eat what he has prepared. He probably has a woman on his side with low self esteem who would give her life to make him happy. If it is true you can judge a person by their history, my visions are as accurate as if I were sprawled out in a lawn chair waiting on the food.

Scooter always advised leaving our environment would not change the person. He could have never been more right. "You can't run from yourself. They don't make cars or shoes that nice for you to outrun your mind." The only thing in my life that has changed is I am happy here just being me. I have lived my entire life with wishing, and yearning for an different outcome. Not anymore, my miseries blends well here with the ghost. I may have realized that I did not run from myself. I ran towards myself. Somehow, I still manage to get lonely with hundreds of thousands of tourist coming in an out. I am comforted to know there are hundreds of thousands of lonely hearts just like mine on these infamous streets that I thought I would only ever see in vampire novels.

In the midst of the French Quarter, nobody gives my wrinkled faded tye dyed t-shirts a second glance. Nobody cares that my shorts do not match or that I have worn them three days in a row. If I am feeling a lack of self confidence, I just put on the most feathered, most bedazzled mask and take long walks blending in with the tourist and the crazies. Here on the West Bank of the city the NA/AA meetings here look more like business events than the dusty church basements I am used to. The only thing that has changed with these meetings is the geography, the accents and the size of the meeting spot. It is still the same protocol, the same sob stories from the demons of their past. The self loathing. The people who have caused their own demise.

And there he stands, the key to my stability to this muggy heat. He may not be anyone else's cup of tea but he is my tall drink of water. His bayou accent disappears as he reads with such authority and such knowledge. He may not know I exist, but he will. He towers over the lectern, reminding me of someone. His round stomach makes it evident he has gave up his wild nights bar hopping on Bourbon Street for chicken wings, corn dogs and Geaux Tigers cheers on Saturdays and faithful Sundays, watching Drew Brees on the big screen. That may pose a problem for me. I make a mental note to text Jewel to pick her brain about all of her knowledge about football. I know nothing at all about sports. But in the south it is a requirement like sugar in tea.

Murray Thibodeaux, he is going to be my everything. I make another mental note to search for a Saints t-shirt so I will appear a fan. I have a while to learn about touchdowns and field goals. Nobody will ask me any particular questions because people already assume everyone knows about penalties and plays. If I get hemmed up in questioning, I will just say "Roll Tide" and keep it moving. Nobody ever questions an Alabama fan. Murray, will not be an easy task to conquer. He may expect me to cook because I am still built like I love to eat. There is enough bakeries in this areas I can appease him with sweets. I do not have Sabra and Myra to advise me. This time I am on my own.

As he speaks of his trials and triumphs keeping everyone focused on the way his mustache bounces as his lips moves. I map out the city in my mind, focusing on the streets that are the most dimly lit. I pay no attention to step five, as I daydream about walking hand in hand

with him down the street. I ponder on taking tinier strides and

wondering if I should put a sway in my hips as we walk. Sexiness has

never came natural to me. I have always been envious of those

women who can wear heels and not tumble down flat on their face.

Dresses never looked feminine on me. They always appear I am a

farmers wife from rural Nebraska in the forties.

Murray, continues on about his studies at Tulane. I knew he was

intelligent. I imagine our conversations while we stroll the sidewalks

passing art shops. French or Spanish architecture? He intrigues me

and I want to know everything about him. I want to be front and

center at the next meeting and make sure he sees me. I think he is

going to be the chicken soup for my soul. I get lonely here

sometimes. I feel like I am a lion that has been tossed from the

pride. I know I left on my own thanks to the advice of Alisha. I was

not running from legal troubles. I did not have legal consequences. I refuse to let my mind reflect back on any bad that Sterling ever did to me.

His memory deserves better than that. His memory with me should be focused on the good years we spent together. I take Sabras advice with me as I begin to set my sights on my new target. When I would confide in her how sad Sterling had started making me feel so sad, ashamed, worthless, she would say "Leave him" I would counter that with "But, I can't I love him." She would say "So, find someone else to love. Get a life." I really wish she were still around so I could interrupt her Gaithers television show she never missed. Or hear her cuss me out for calling interrupting Andy Griffith. She only watched those shows every single time there aired. She would be proud if she could see me now. Maybe, she would not be so proud. Sabra always had a way of having a totally opposite reaction than I expected her to have. She may be looking down from whatever cloud she is planted on saying "Muffy, that is so stupid just give up on men." The only men in our family are the ones who were born with our last names is for a reason. We are dominant females.

Like a bullseye on a target I keep my mind on Murray. I embrace my daydreams. I plan on being docile. I make plans with him to be in front of the Louisiana Supreme Court strolling beside of the black wrought iron fencing, while I listen to whatever hopes and dreams he wants to share with me. The only flaw with these plans are he does not know about them. After the meeting wraps up I slip out too coy to introduce myself.

Before, I head to the Louisburg apartment complex that I now call home, I make it to Sonic just slightly before the happy hour rush comes in. I am talking to Sterling and Alisha as I place my order. The high pitched annoying voice through the speaker says "Ma'am can you repeat that. It is hard for me to hear you." Loudly I repeat. "Supersonic bacon double cheeseburger with a strawberry shake." The high pitched voice snidely says "Will that be all? "Yes, thank you" she blabs my total that I pay zero attention to the amount.

And continue my conversation. That should have been that simple.

However, she says. "Will y'all be sharing?" I began to ask her who

added with a bunch of expletives be sharing what.

They skate out with my food. But now I want to fight. I feel invited

to fight because there are two of them. When has sonic ever sent

out two people to give a one bag order? I open my car door and get

eye to eye with the tiny waisted ugly face teen. "Give me my food.

Or get your ass beat all over this parking lot. The dark skin girl

bracing herself in her roller blades starts to giggle. I throw the

money on the ground and snatch the bag and my drink. "What is so

funny? Do you not believe I can beat both of y'all at the same time."

It is moments like this I hate my life.

As they spin their skates I hear one talk to the other. "Oh my God,

there wasn't even nobody in that car with her, who was she talking

to?" They giggle. I hate to be laughed at. What was so funny? I

resist the urge to snatch them up. Over the years, I have gained composure. I think about consequences more. Especially without Jewel close by to bond me out if need be. I still speed off burning rubber into the pavement. I want to put this car in reverse a plow them tiny terrorist down to their death. I keep going swerving and chewing while I practice what I am going to say when I call their district manager tomorrow.

I have learned the hard way that in-house managers rarely reprimand their employees. They do not want to deal with them either. I am not happy about their lack of respect for me. I am not about to let them get away with it. I almost collide into the sidewalk as I park my car. I jump out and breathe in the humidity. I am not used to March nights feeling this warm. This is so amazing to my soul. I will live here fifty years and every time I feel this weather kiss me it will feel like the first time.

CHAPTER TWENTY FOUR

The weather may have changed along with my zip code. My messy living has remained the same. Jewel calls me a few times a week as if she is a meddling mother in law. "Muffy, are you cleaning? Muffy, Are you taking your trash out. Muffy, Are you taking your medicine?" She goes on to warn me about the risk of roaches living in the south, also living in an apartment complex. She says she just worries that if a neighbor of mine gets them they will take up breeding in my filth. I always lie and tell her that I am doing all that I am supposed to do. That was working well until she has to decided to overstep meddling to the overbearing point. "Muffy, I think I need to start video chatting with you. That way I can watch you take your medicine." I do not know what she thinks this Prozac is really going to do for me. Except make me eat and sleep. Jewell, thinks her meddling is just her trying to be helpful. I am not the only one who does not like to video chat with her. We worry she is paying more attention to our background than our face.

I need Ativan that is what helps me but, I have no degree in psychiatry. Doctors do not listen to what I know will help me. I can not go in the office and be honest. I can not tell them about how I have to live my life distrusting reality. Last night when I stepped into the bathroom I caught a glimpse of Sterling in the mirror. They would dope me up and I would not be able to work. I like when Alisha and Sterling visit me. It helps me with the lonesomeness. They see me as a crazy lady pill shopping. I do not want to return back home like a scalded dog. I want to stay here and find true love and success. I have a job at a call center. The pay is decent. I do not have much money left over but its enough.

My apartment has been furnished with thrift store finds. When I first got here all I had was an air bed. I have no television. There is no need for the added expense of cable. Besides, I would rather read or chat for hours on the phone. My bland beige walls are as bare as they were before I got the key. I live on the bottom floor so that helps me tremendously. I still lack motivation for physical activity. Despite my lack of self confidence I took the initiative to sign this lease. I was growing tired of sleeping in my car in parking lots. I still desire to get high, but I have yet to discover where to shop for that at. The only thing that will make my life full will be when Murray notices me.

Jewel, recommends that I only focus on myself. Where is the fun in that? She is my life coach and I respect her opinion that is as far as that goes. Allison, calls me quite often. We laugh and talk for hours. She tells me secrets about her life and swears me to secrecy. Of course, I repeat them to all that I think is interested. One miraculous story that I share with anyone who has ears is she no longer waste money or her life getting high. Perhaps we were cursed with those demons of addiction and low self esteem. Funny thing is we are still the same people dealing with the same problems but we are not medicating the same way. No lengthy stays in rehabilitation facilities only our mindset. We have been prisoners in our own minds.

I rush from work and fight this traffic. Road rage. How have I not killed me or someone else? I drive on the shoulder of the road going a tad bit over the speed limit to avoid forty minutes of rush hour, reading license plates and looking at tail lights. Everyday, I deal with some rude driver who refuses to let me over when it is time to put my wheels back on the pavement. I have to be aggressive and punch it. My lead foot slamming onto the gas pedal. Each day I hear horns blaring at me and sometimes foul language being yelled at me. I keep going. But not without hurling the same words back in their direction.

Today's drive home I had something to look forward to. I drove a lot faster and cursed back a little less. I rushed in my empty apartment tossing what was in my pockets on the couch. I jumped in the shower for a few minutes. I was in there so less amount of time the

water barely hit my hair. I slipped my tshirt over my head and slid

up my shorts. It took me fifteen minutes for me to find the keys I

had just laid down. They were in between the couch cushions. I

thought for sure someone had came inside while I was in the

shower and took them. I ranted and screamed and cussing until the

jingle of the keys were in my hand.

Tonight is another meeting where Murray will be a speaker. Work,

nor traffic was going to prevent me from being here on time. Before

we begin, everyone is so friendly toward me. I feel so welcomed.

Perhaps the last time I was here I was a phantom. I do not recall all

of this outpouring of southern charm. Murray, walks in. His nose

points downward as if he has Lebanese in his gene pool. He

introduces himself and makes a joke. It is not funny, but I laugh

anyway. The windows to his soul are deep brown. I see we share

the same misdirection and loneliness. I wonder if he too, sees

things that are not real. I wonder if when he went to his mother telling her about his visions did she accuse him of drug use like mine

did as a teenager. No, that is wishful thinking. He does not have one

wrinkle in his creased shirt. His cologne is not a familiar smell to me.

It must be expensive.

He has his life together. He is teaching from an iPad not a book.

Because of my past experiences I can not help but to wonder if his

creased shirt, iPad and expensive cologne was paid for by the price

of a woman's love for him, like so many men of my past. I wonder if

he had to work at his perfection or does perfection come naturally

to him like crazy does to me. During the intermission giraffe like

strides comes closer to me. I feel a euphoria buzzing him by brain as

he reaches out his soft hand to shake my sweaty palm. How

embarrassing? I can not even shake a hand without goofing up. He

pretends that he does not even notice. "You must be new in town, I

have not seen you around." I cast him a sheepish smile, "I am new

here." Someone else grabs his attention. He is looking at me as he

is talking to them.

He must have found me intriguing. After the meeting wrapped up, he invited me to meet him for coffee. Coffee, at night? I do not drink it morning or night. I am not that concerned with the caffeine rituals of coffee beans. My obsession became a fast reality as we sit eye gazing at Starbucks. I never want this night to end. We get to know each other by asking questions. Ever been married? How many children? Where are you from? First date questions. This is a date. I am so excited I am shaking my leg to remain seated. Murray, tells me that he has been widowed. He goes on to say he is seven years clean. I lie to him about giving birth. Technically it was not a lie. He asked "How many children do you have? I said "None." He did not ask if I had ever given birth. Not, a lie. I gave my children away and the right to be called mother went with them.

Murray, is not handsome. His personality is gorgeous. I have been laughing this entire evening. He is intelligent. He is street savvy. Murray, is everything but beautiful. He is beautiful to me. His wisdom, his plight to overcome his demons is reminiscent of

Sterling. He has not even finished sipping grande black coffee and I

am already head over heels. I can only hope I do not snort laughter

at the jokes he is telling me. He finds me witty as well. This coffee

and fountain drink date is way better than any bar I have been in.

I rush to get for work at his place. I google directions from his house

to the call center. He tidies up the bed while I am still in it. It was a

good night and now he is ruining the morning waking up an hour

before the alarm goes off to clean. The accolades of his affection

has me feeling like I am walking on sunshine. His tiny apartment is

so spotless the only reason you can see anyone lives here is the art

gallery of pictures of his family hanging on the walls. He told me he

had fathered six children. After last night I see why. All of his

children are grown now. A lonely bachelor. He does not have to

worry about any longer. I will do everything in my power to stay by

his side.

CHAPTER TWENTY FIVE

I can not believe the course of events that has happened. A few
weeks ago I was the one sleeping in his bed. I have been sleeping
there twice a week ever since. Tonight, a slender red head takes my
place. I did not do anything to him to deserve this. He told me he
wanted to be with me. The only wrongdoing I have done was
believe him. I should have known someone like him could not love
me. He made me believe he could. I am not going to stop until he
does. I am parked outside with my headlights on high beam glowing
right through the living room. Neither of them care to come
outside. The glare of my headlights is casting a glow too bright for
me to see what is going inside.

I will wait here for days if I have to until she comes outside. How dare her try to take my place. Does she know about me? Would she care if she did? Probably not. My mind races as if it is curving laps at Talladega Speedway. I call Jewel, but it is too late for her to pick up. I call Allison. I should have brought a snack. It looks like I am going to be here awhile. Allison, tries to rationalize with me. "Muffy, go home, you have worked so hard. Please stop this. Pull out and go home." I do not want to listen to her. I do not want to go home. I want Murrays attention. The attention he is giving the red head.

Allisons pleas continues. I listen. I want to listen. I can not, just leave. He told me that I had a mysterious charm about me. That red headed tramp had to have thrown herself at him. He seemed so perfect. He seemed to be the one. Allison scrambles searching for the statement that will influence me to put this car in reverse. I want to floor it forward. She reminds me that waking up in the morning in a jail cell can result in me losing my job. Losing everything I have worked for. I do not have much. What I have, I have worked to get and worked harder to maintain. A split decision can risk it all.

I know that I have matured. I consider consequences now. I have weighed all of the options. I get out of my car. I pace around my car still weighing if the risk is worth the consequence. I continue to circle my car like a great white shark swimming around a fishing boat. My pride just will not let this go. Doing nothing means I am accepting defeat. That is not in my nature. I promise Allison I will not hurt anyone as I dig through the trash in my backseat feeling for the metal of the Louisville slugger. I raise it up as if I had discovered a sword. I swing the bat into the windshield to the car parked to my left. His car. I can hear Sabra talking to me just as clear as if she were leaning over my shoulder. "Muffy you have always surrounded yourself with losers. What do you expect? For years I have told you decent men do not dwell in the bottom of the barrel." Her words anger me fueling my fire to force the bat to kiss the rear windshield. Through, the shatters of glass I hear the front door open.

I am too panicked to lift my eyes in that direction. I know they are going to call the police and I am going to be arrested. I jump back in my car as if Bo Duke taught me how to drive. I speed off into the night. I honestly do not feel he should have me arrested. He deserves this. I rush into my apartment locking the door behind me. I am out of breath. I still get enough wind to call Jewel. Determined to wake her up I call three times before she answers. "Don't cuss me out! Don't be mad!" I pant. Jewel taught us years ago even when she was a drug dealer only call after nine o'clock at night if you are dead. Do not even dial at 8:58pm. I do not expect her to understand. Her husband is a demon but he is not a cheater. Much to my surprise she says. "Way to go Muffy, it is high time in life you stop cowering down to men and allowing them to do you any kind of way with no repercussions." She giggles and ask "Did he come outside?" I tell her how I left as soon as I heard the front door open.

"That is probably the best thing for him to do. Just stay safe and let you be crazy." I am still in fear that the police is going to pound on my door. Our conversation shifts from my crazy antics to the crazy antics of the people that I once called neighbors. Gossiping with Jewel will never be as fun as when I spent countless hours on the phone gossiping with Alisha. Jewel, is not nearly as judgmental. And she always repeats what has been based on facts not hearsay. Before we hang up Jewel pauses and says "Muffy, I would have done the exact same thing." It comforts me to know she is still a little ornery.

A light mist of rain has graced the city this morning. I am stable with my thoughts. I am ready to go to work and let my coworkers know about my adventures of last night. They always get a kick out of the stories. Of course there are a few skeptics that believe my insanity is not real. Oh how I wish they were right. I can not go back and change anything and I am not so sure that I would if I could. I am happy here. Often times grateful for the broken road that brought me this far. Many of life's lesson I have to keep learning. The one I will never have to retrain on is alcohol. I am living in a city where alcohol is part of the tourism. It is as much as a daily routine as brushing your teeth but I know better. The rush for me is fabulous at first. The drinking without thinking, my favorite part, the speaking without the thinking.

The down side happened as the liquor flowed through my veins, making its way to my not so stable brain. Adverse effect on me. Others drink for fun or to kill a pain in their soul. It pacifies them but not for me. I experience a black out phase where I am not asleep. Fully awake and unaware of my actions. The voices instruct me to harm myself. They become in sync and all agreeing that I should take my anger out on myself. They are persistent in telling me the only way they will shut up is if death comes. I drank more to drown them out. That only resulted in them being louder and screeching the advice for me to cut deeper into my skin.

On the way home from work with the car vibrating on the rumbler pipes on the shoulder of the road. It dawns on me there is another meeting scheduled for tonight. I want to go. I need to see the look on his face. I wonder if he will even show up and if that tawdry red head will be on his arm. I am not going to sit back and do nothing and allow them the happiness I feel I deserve with him. I can not decide how to make my move. Show up early. Make an entrance showing up late. I am certainly showing up. Will I leave handcuffed? That shall be determined based on their actions. Distracted from driving by the ringing of my cell phone. I glance down contemplating on ignoring it until I safely merge. Sparked by curiously I peek to see who is calling me. MURRAY all caps with a heart emoji after his name is lighting up my screen. Moved by impulse I slide to answer.

92.3 FM and noise from the traffic muffles his voice. I am too uncoordinated to hold the phone and turn down the radio. I go against my nature and do it anyway. Dropping the phone in the floor and turning the volume the opposite way blaring the voice of Chris Chaos through the speakers. With the car still in motion I take my eyes off of the road and pick the phone up causing me to just miss a Kia Soul by less than an inch. Their horn blows as I tap the power button on the radio. I need to hear clearly what he has to say. "Muffy, I need to see you tonight after the meeting. Please meet with me." His sincerity continues as he tells me where to meet him. He asked me not to attend tonight's meeting. My loneliness drives me to doing just as he instructs. At 8:20 on the dot I arrive at the El Paso Mexican Grill. I feel delighted he chose this place to meet. He remembered when I told him that burritos was one of the joys in life I can not live without.

I paid attention to his thoughtfulness as he pulled in a few spaces down from where I had parked. We step onto the sidewalk together. My Birkenstock flaps on the edge of the sidewalk causing me to stumble a bit. Aggravated with my clumsiness I let the F-bomb fly from my lips. Murray, smiles impressed that I am so uncouth I curse in public. He has already mentioned my rawness

makes me a diamond to him. We walk in together and wait to be

seated. He speaks to the hostess in fluent Spanish. I am impressed.

They seat us in a booth in the back. As the mariachi band plays love

songs I can not understand Murray starts his explanation. "I am

taking full responsibility for my actions last night. I should have told

you I was expecting company and why. I deserved it." I take in his

apology like a bee seething honey. He goes to explain how nothing

happened with that tawdry red head. He did not refer to her like

that. I paid no attention to the name of the skank. She was only

there as a friend. He told me if I had have knocked on the door

instead of losing my whole mind I could have came inside.

"Muffy, that behavior is not acceptable." I apologized and promised

to never overreact again. We laughed some more and I thanked him

graciously for his forgiveness and understanding. Our night

continued on until the next morning. This is where I want to be

forever. In this city, with this man, in this apartment. Murray, is an excellent cook. His stove looks brand new. He cleans it as soon as he is done cooking. Sometimes wiping before it has even cooled off. He washes his dishes as he goes. As soon as we eat at his kitchen table he is back at the sink washing. I have offered to help although I did not really want to. I was relieved when he told me no just relax. He sweeps his while ceramic tile floors making it look as good as new.

His clean apartment reminds me of how my mother kept house. I feel at home here. So when he suggested that we become an item. I gladly gave up my address and moved in with him. I have always carried myself. Even when the load was too heavy for my shoulders to bare. I made a way to care for myself. I wanted to make a good impression so I have started paying the water bill and the power bill. It seems like the more I make the more it takes to live here. Jewel, says that I need to have a nest egg if something happens. Of course, I do not listen. Just like when I moved from my apartment she told me to clean it spotless. I did not. The apartment manager called and asked me how long had I been living in those squalor conditions. She told me there would be no chance that I will get my deposit back.

Murray, works in the heating and air conditioning business. He does electrical work on the side. We laugh about how he can fix anything but I can not even fix a can of soup. I had no idea you have to add water. I should read instructions. My lack of domestic abilities is wearing on his nerves. He gives me cleaning chore list, which I do not complete. He does not like the way that I fold clothes. He claims "There are more wrinkles after you fold them than when left in the dryer." He nitpicks about the way I sweep. He claims "You are supposed to start the broom by the wall and sweep toward the center of the floor." All of these lessons become too much for me. I have told him from the beginning I am a bread winner not a maid. He was not going for that since he makes twice as much money as I do.

His fits of rage, over his lair causes me stress. Everything could not be more perfect, until he sees a mess. I left my plate in the microwave with the intention of going back and finishing later. I forgot all about it for a few days. Murray, accused me of hiding dishes like a child to avoid having to wash them. His strong voice vibrated the windows as he yelled what a lazy cow I was. He charged toward me. A familiar scenario. He lifted my plump body off of the floor, using my hair as a handle. He got nose to nose with me. He told me that I was too nasty and I had to leave. He released his hands dropping me. He opened the door and demanded that I "Get out and never comeback." I began to sob and explain "I had nowhere else to go." That was a fact that did not matter to him. "Muffy, get out before I throw you out on your tail."

I would not budge. I jumped up into his face, daring him to hit me like a man. I blurted out more expletives telling him how only a punk would hit a woman. As he dragged me to the opened door he said "You are no woman." He slammed the door behind me, leaving me with nowhere to stay and no money to get a room for the night. I called Jewel. I was wailing and crying. She was not sympathetic. "Muffy, I told you to save at least fifty dollars a week. You never know someone until you live with them. And I have told you to start cleaning up after yourself." She still does not understand that I would spend every cent to be loved. She still does not understand I hate to clean. It makes me feel dirty to scrape food off of a plate. She did, help with me with brainstorming on a place to stay. "What about your friend, you talk about? Can you stay with her?" I explain to her I can stay with Montana but I do not want to. I want to stay in the apartment with Murray.

Montana would have welcomed me with open arms. I chose to drive around until my gas light came on. I met Montana at a NA meeting, our friendship sparked. She has represented a motherly mentor for me since day one. She is always advising me on things I could care less about like credit, savings and eating well. I live to eat. Montana, eats to live. She explains the difference but the only thing I pay attention to is she does not eat fast food. I tend to lose interest in things when it is not what I want to hear. I called her and told her about the fight Murray and I just had. Just like I thought she would say. "Come stay with me." Do not get me wrong she is great people, but I want to stay with my great man. I can see how my messiness annoys him. I take full responsibility for the whole incident.

The rain is battering the pavement. I hate torrential down pours here. Everyone else feels the cooler weather in the aftermath slightly before the oven temperature humidity sets in. They embrace what Mother Nature sends. I only see the rain hammering and visions of the news clips when hurricane Katrina came through. I see bus loads of people in the Astro dome. My heart full of feat and panic. I call Murray. He declines my call so I redial and redial until I hear him say "Hello." A moment of silence as I swallow my tears back. "I want to come back, I promise I will clean everyday." He says. "You are insulting my intelligence you are not going to do what you are incapable of doing, I do not mind to clean. But I will not live in filth, I had six children, not one of them were as nasty as you." He can hear my whimpers. "Muffy, you can come back but I do not want to live like that. You pushed too far." My tires splash through the water as I make my way back. He opens the door to me looking like a drowned horse. He cunningly smiles at me and reaches his arms around me. Neither of us make mention of the incident any further.

The more the days turned into weeks the more I grew concerned that there is great possibility that no one on earth will ever understand me like Sterling did. Murray has planted a seed of fear in me. His too frequent cruel words waters it. I shower even less now. I have thoughts that he is going to come in the bathroom and throw hot grease on me. I am only under the water less than two minutes. I am afraid of falling and him holding me down until I drown. The voices in my mind feel the same way. At this point it is hard for me to tell what is real and what the demons in my mind

are saying.

Montana, says I should run like a triathlon champion. I have told her

a lot about myself as we shared our upbringings and life in general. I

have kept the demons in my mind confidential. She has divulged

her darkest secrets to me but I have kept my lips sealed. I told her

about Sterling but she believes it was suicide. Technically it was. It

seems as if Montana and me have been friends our entire life. But

how can I form the words that I see things that are not real. I hear

things that are absurd. In my past when I have confided in people

they have laughed it off. Or accused me of faking for attention. One

time a friend even implied that I was some sort of a medium. The

reason people can not fathom how my mind ticks backwards is

because I can keep a job. I have an erudite vocabulary. I am

loquacious. So nobody ever gives it a second thought. They blame

my irresponsibility's on the drug phase. They rarely recognize my imprudent actions were long before I ever leaned my face down on a dollar bill.

CHAPTER TWENTY SIX

My first Mardi Gras. I needed this in my life twenty years ago. Murray and I scrambled through the sea of people on St. Charles Avenue. When the parade began to glide past my heart fluttered. The decadent detail of each float. They have gave life to an idea. These Krewes tell a story. Watching this is as if words from pages have came to life before your eyes. Beads are being tossed. I so desperately want to lift my shirt and earn my beads. Since I am sober and I am getting beads anyway, there is no need to shock the crowd. Murray and I are walking hand in hand as we make our way to Bourbon Street. I can barely hear him through the music, through the laughter. There is no doubt I am the only sober person on this street. The party goes on street after street. Trumpets blowing I can not help but to have a rhythmless dance in the small space I have. A wedding party marches by and I snap blurry pictures. I eat pizza by the slice and Murray he drinks Grenades. His sobriety abruptly ended on Fat Tuesday.

He drinks until he loses consciousness. That is if I am lucky. He slobbers and slurs. Disgusting. His violence has got worse. And we never make mention of it in the aftermath. My violence has accelerated. I do not cower down and allow him to beat on me. I fight back. The more Grenades Murray drinks the more energetic he becomes. I am tired and ready to go back to the apartment. I continue to walk with him with my feet swelling out of my Birkenstocks. My steps become painful and he cusses me for being overweight and out of shape. Murrays words always make me feel so useless and unloved. His actions toward me do the same since he traded AA meetings for Crown Royal. A couple of hours later, my feet are so swollen they have resistance as I try to bend my feet to take steps. The burning from the swelling makes me feel as though I have a thousand bees stinging the arches of my feet. Murray is staggering as he turns the key to open the door. I greet the couch like a long lost pal. I throw my legs up on the back to elevate them. "Get your nasty feet off of the back of my couch!" He demands before he falls face first on the floor. I panic for a second at the thud his body made as it hit. Then I hear him snoring. I roll my eyes his direction and continue on with my moments of relaxation. I start to read Interview with a Vampire. This is close to the hundredth time I have read this story. It seems so much more exciting to me this time because, I am reading it in the city where it was written in. My senses of entertainment is combined with an odd sense of privilege.

I am not far into the fifth chapter when Murray rolls over moaning. I notice his nose is busted up from his fall. I have made this man feel like he was somebody only for him to make me feel like a nobody. Before his voice raises, the demons in my mind start whispering. I can not understand what they are saying. All of them whispering at once as if they talking to me from underwater. I lay my book aside and stare at Murray while he fumbles to raise his large body from the tile. It is only four o'clock in the afternoon and I can feel the tension of a late night bar room brawl. I grab my carnevale mask and place it on my face. I have no idea why I am wearing a mask while I am waiting to get tossed like a rag doll. I am aware of my actions yet unaware of the reasoning. I brace my feet as he rises up like a boxer on a mission arising from the ring. There is no referee or corner man here to protect me from the blows.

I walk to the door as I open it I get pulled backwards. I feel his hands tightly around my throat. I know I am going to die today. I will be damned if I give him the powers to take the life I have fought for a half of century to keep. I do not resist the choking. I know that will make it worse. His grip gets tighter. With my free hands I reach out and grab his manhood. The tighter he squeezes my throat. The tighter I squeeze. I see the expression on his face, but his words are muted to me. He releases his grip. Instead of me walking on out of the door. I close it and lock it. I scream in his face. "I am tired today. After, today you will never put your hands on another woman!" I can hear his evil laugh and him say to me. "YOU ARE NO WOMAN." I agree with him. "YOU ARE RIGHT I AM THE DEVIL." I did not mean to say that and when I heard the words coming out of my mouth I was as shocked as he was. I do not feel possessed but I do feel like fighting. Winning for once.

I put my fingers in his eyeballs and press in with all of my might. I leap forward letting his eyeballs lift the entire weight of my body. He shakes his head slinging me. But I do not let go. I knee him in his manhood and he stumbles back. It folds him like a bad hand of poker. He coughs. He does not hit me back and if he does I do not feel his punches. I am numb all over. I am fighting him for every woman he has ever hit. I am fighting him for every woman who has loved a man that made them feel like a nothing. Less than human. I knee him in his manhood once more. He showed the weakness there so I am going to continue to knee him. This time it knocks him over onto the floor. I stomp him while he is down. He is still to intoxicated to be fast enough to grab my legs. But he tries. I take my foot and slam it into his mouth. I scream "Shut Up!" Although I did not even hear what he is saying. I still hear these vicious whispers.

I reach over and grab the fireplace shovel. I have not touched a shovel since the day I found my baby sisters remains. The iron of the shovel smashes against his temple. Blood splatters. The sight of the blood panics me. I pound again and again until his face is unrecognizable. I do not hear his moans. The expressions on his face show excruciating pain. This inspires me to hit him again and again. His breathing is slowing. He reaches up as if he is needing help. I grab his hand and lay it back to his side. I take the shovel as if I am digging into the earth and drive it into his hand.

I am exhausted once more. What a great day we could have had. What a great life we could have made together. He continued to use me and take advantage of my love. Disregarding my feelings. Now, I am watching him die over it. I wonder if he thinks mistreating me is still okay now. I wonder if he feels strong for all of the times he jerked my hair out by the root. I watch a thin cloud of vapor rise up from his mouth. I am guessing that is his soul leaving his body. If that is true it went the opposite way of where it was supposed to travel.

I take my place back on the couch. Instead of finishing my novel I am staring in wonderment as I look at his lifeless body. I did not mean to kill Sterling. I was defending myself. I really believed he was going to kill me. I did not mean to kill Robert, and still to this day I am unsure of how I did it. As years rolled past visions haunt me and I see him running for his life. I sometimes feel the jolt when the SUV tapped against his body. At times I will see visions of his body bouncing off of the hood and I feel the thud as the tires crushed him. I am unsure of if I killed him. What happened to his body when I went back to look? Murray, is different I did mean to

kill him. I enjoyed every moan that I heard him exhale.

Perhaps due to my mental illness abusive men are drawn to me like

a magnet. They must know to seek me out. At first they seem

smitten with my level of crazy. Then they begin to feed off of my

vulnerabilities like a maggot sucking on garbage bags left behind by

picnickers in the summertime. Looking at Murrays face it is a real

life account of how my heart feels. It is so easy for other people to

move on when bad things happen to them. Not for me. It never has

been. No matter how well I clean myself up, when I see my

reflection I hear the taunts and chants from the playground children

during my childhood.

Fear slowly seeps through my body. It is time for me to figure out

the what is my next move. Dreaded thoughts I rarely choose the

right answer to. I can not just leave him in the floor. His children will

come looking for him if he misses a day without calling. If they do not get drunk text from their father they may get suspicious. I reach for his cellphone and text "Hey, lets have dinner Friday." To three of the six of them. I feel a sense of guilt for taking their father away from them. Mean to me, mean to their mothers yet, he was never mean to them. Four boys, two girls. All of them grew up to make something of themselves. They loved him. He loved them. There is no doubt in my mind they are not going to stop until I am on death row. They never knew him the way I did or their mothers did.

I can stage a scene to make it look like he was robbed. I doubt anyone will suspect I was strong enough to to overpower and beat a man bigger than me to a brutal death. How will that help me for the next time I feel loneliness? And end up in the same situation again. I could hide him under the bed. But I do not love him enough to hold on to him the way I did Sterling. On crime shows on television they always show a woman motivated to kill for insurance money. Who writes the scripts for women like me who kill because they get tired? Who airs the stories when people like me allow the demons in others to bring out their demonic spirits.

I can not look at his gruesome face any longer. I have to get out of here. I grab the keys and jump in my car. I drive to nowhere but end up on Canal Street. I just follow slowly behind the traffic. Once more taking in the views. I look at license plates of the cars that surround me. IROL4TDE with an Alabama plate. I end up behind a large SUV with a sparkly sticker in the rear windshield Spoiled by a WV Miner. There's a silhouette of a miner on the sticker. The tag reads DRTY$. I follow behind Dirty Money until they turn off to Harrahs. I keep straight.

I make my way through the crowd. I walk until I am leaning on the rail of the point of no return. I look down at the churning brown waters of the Mississippi. I resist the urge to call Jewel. I know hearing her voice will make me weak. I need to be strong. I think about all of the great things this river has brought to the country.

Mostly I think about how this murky water bleeds into a emerald green ocean. It is hard to focus on this river and not have a second of thought about Mark Twain. The voices start back. I hear them tell me how disappointed my mom and dad would be if they were alive to witness the fate that lays in my future. They continue to tell me Sabra is cackling at my stupidity. How she could understand if he really threw hot grease on me. But for me to fear a thought. Is insane. I scream "Shut up." They do not listen. I scream again and again but they only get louder. The noises in my mind have seized the background noises in my reality. My body aches so bad. Intense pain radiating throughout my muscles. Murray, was not an easy fight.

I no longer want to experience physical pain. I am older now. It is time for me to give my body peace. I no longer want demons plaguing my mind. I am hopeless that I will find someone who does not cause pain to my heart. I hope God forgives me. Even though I never could forgive him for making me defective. I had everything handed to me except for sanity. Without another thought I dive in. The cold water stings my skin. The water blankets over me. I go deeper and deeper. I do not want to do this. I pray it is not too late. The currents have swallowed me up. The way the water is beating my body. I know it is too late. I fight the water with all of my might. Vigorously flailing my arms to hold on to my life. Living was not as hard as dying this way. Somehow I thought it would be peaceful.

I feel my arms getting weaker, although I try to lift them I have no strength left. Water enters through my gasping screams. The water has blurred my vision. I only hear death by drowning, I can not see it anymore. I see angels. I do not want to go with them. I need to be saved. I utter OH GOD PLEASE SAVE ME. My prayers are going unanswered. I fight violently to live. I just want to live no matter if it is on death row. More flailing my arms, although no movement is happening. I feel myself getting so sleepy. I am not giving up. I will fight. And when I am pulled from this mistake I will do better. I will make something of my life and the years that remain.

An overwhelming sense of euphoria embraces me as the angels get

closer. They bring with them a sense of peace. This is the peace I

have always desired. I am going home. The life I leave behind is not

worth fighting for. I am finished. I do not feel my body being

readjusted to the way the wind blows the water. Everything is dark

and quiet. Serene.

SYNOPSIS

When Facts meet fiction, this story is based on true events. Muffy Concord, survives through a precarious life with the ambition of finding true love and adoration. Muffy's plight seems unattainable as she meets one Mr. Wrong after another. After years of living in a state of confusion due to her variety of mental illnesses, she meets the man of her dreams. Years pass before she realizes the man of her dreams is really the man of her worst nightmares. Muffy, battles on demons of addiction and mental disorders as she figures out what she must do to obtain happiness.

About the Author

Born in a small southern West Virginian town. Lori realized she was

surrounded by stories to good not to share. For years she wrote as

a hobby to pass any free time she had while raising her two

daughters. Lori Ann, now lives in Pelham, Alabama where she works

as a freelance paraglegal.

i

Made in the USA
Columbia, SC
06 February 2023

11139070R00191